François the Waif

GEORGE SAND

Translated by
JANE MINOT SEDGWICK

RENARD PRESS

RENARD PRESS LTD

124 City Road
London EC1V 2NX
United Kingdom
info@renardpress.com
020 8050 2928

www.renardpress.com

François the Waif first published in French as *François le Champi* in 1848
This translation by Jane Minot Sedgwick first published in 1894
This edition first published by Renard Press Ltd in 2024

Edited text and Notes © Renard Press Ltd, 2024

Cover design by Will Dady, adapted from Arthur Mackmurdo's cover for *Wren's City Churches* (Kent: G. Allen, 1883)

Printed and bound in the UK on carbon-balanced papers by CMP Books

ISBN: 978-1-80447-102-9

9 8 7 6 5 4 3 2 1

CLIMATE POSITIVE   Renard Press is proud to be a climate positive publisher, removing more carbon from the air than we emit and planting a small forest. For more information see renardpress.com/eco.

CONTENTS

PREFATORY NOTE

François le Champi, a pretty idyll that tells of homely affections, self-devotion, 'humble cares and delicate fears', opens a little vista into that Arcadia to which, the poet says, we were all born. It offers many difficulties to the translator. It is a rustic tale, put into the mouths of peasants, who relate it with a primitive simplicity, sweet and full of sentiment in the French, but prone to degenerate into mawkishness and monotony when turned into English. Great care has been taken to keep the English of this version simple and idiomatic, and yet religiously to avoid any breach of faith towards the author. It is hoped that, though the original pure and limpid waters have necessarily contracted some stain by being forced into another channel, they may yet yield refreshment to those thirsty souls who cannot seek them at the fountainhead.

J.M.S.

Stockbridge, January 1894

PREFACE

François le Champi appeared for the first time in the feuilleton of the *Journal des débats*.* Just as the plot of my story was reaching its development, another more serious development was announced in the first column of the same newspaper. It was the final downfall of the July Monarchy, in the last days of February 1848.*

This catastrophe was naturally very prejudicial to my story, the publication of which was interrupted and delayed, and not finally completed, if I remember correctly, until the end of a month. For those of my readers who are artists, either by profession or instinct, and are interested in the details of the construction of works of art, I shall add to my introduction that, some days before the conversation of which that introduction is the outcome, I took a walk through the Chemin aux Napes. The word *nape*, which, in the figurative language of that part of the country, designates the beautiful plant called nénufar, or *Nymphaea*,* is happily descriptive of the broad leaves that lie upon the surface of the water, as a cloth (*nappe*) upon a table; but I prefer to write it with a single *p*, and to trace its derivation from *napée*, thus leaving unchanged its mythological origin.

The Chemin aux Napes, which probably none of you, my dear readers, will ever see, as it leads to nothing that can repay you for the trouble of passing through so much mire, is a breakneck path, skirting along a ditch where, in the muddy water, grow the most beautiful nymphaea in the world, more fragrant than lilies, whiter than camellias, purer than the vesture of virgins, in the midst of the lizards and other reptiles that crawl about the mud and flowers, while the kingfisher darts like living lightning along the banks, and skims with a fiery track the rank and luxuriant vegetation of the sewer.

A child six or seven years old, mounted bareback upon a loose horse, made the animal leap the hedge behind me, and then, letting himself slide to the ground, left his shaggy colt in the pasture, and returned to try jumping over the barrier which he had so lightly crossed on horseback a minute before. It was not such an easy task for his little legs; I helped him, and had with him a conversation similar to that between the miller's wife and the foundling, related in the beginning of *The Waif*. When I questioned him about his age, which he did not know, he literally delivered himself of the brilliant reply that he was two years old. He knew neither his own name, nor that of his parents, nor of the place he lived in; all that he knew was to cling on an unbroken colt, as a bird clings to a branch shaken by the storm.

I have had educated several foundlings of both sexes, who have turned out well physically and morally. It is no less certain, however, that these forlorn children are apt, in rural districts, to become bandits, owing to their utter lack of education. Entrusted to the care of the poorest people, because of the insufficient pittance assigned to them, they often practise, for the benefit of their adopted parents, the shameful calling of beggars.* Would it not be possible to increase this pittance on condition that the foundlings shall never beg, even at the doors of their neighbours and friends?

I have also learned by experience that nothing is more difficult than to teach self-respect and the love of work to children who have already begun understandingly to live upon alms.

GEORGE SAND
Nohant, 20th May 1852

FRANÇOIS THE WAIF

INTRODUCTION

R ———— AND I WERE coming home from our walk by the light of the moon, which faintly silvered the dusky country lanes. It was a mild autumn evening, and the sky was slightly overcast; we observed the resonance of the air peculiar to the season, and a certain mystery spread over the face of nature. At the approach of the long winter sleep, it seems as if every creature and thing stealthily agreed to enjoy what is left of life and animation before the deadly torpor of the frost; and as if the whole creation, in order to cheat the march of time, and to avoid being detected and interrupted in the last frolics of its festival, advanced without sound or apparent motion towards its orgies in the night. The birds give out stifled cries instead of their joyous summer warblings. The cricket of the fields sometimes chirps inadvertently; but it soon stops again, and carries elsewhere its song or its wail. The plants hastily breathe out their last perfume, which is all the sweeter for being more delicate and less profuse. The yellowing leaves now no longer rustle in the breeze, and the flocks and herds graze in silence without cries of love or combat.

My friend and I walked quietly along, and our involuntary thoughtfulness made us silent and attentive to the softened beauty of nature, and to the enchanting harmony of her last chords, which were dying away in an imperceptible pianissimo. Autumn is a sad and sweet andante, which makes an admirable preparation for the solemn adagio of winter.*

'It is all so peaceful,' said my friend at last, for, in spite of our silence, he had followed my thoughts as I followed his; 'everything seems absorbed in a reverie so foreign and so indifferent to the labours, cares and preoccupations of man, that I wonder what expression, what colour and what form of art and poetry human intelligence could give at this moment to the face of nature. In order to explain better to you the end of my inquiry, I may compare the evening, the sky and the landscape, dimmed, and yet harmonious and complete, to the soul of a wise and religious peasant, who labours and profits by his toil, who rejoices in the possession of the life to which he is born, without the need, the longing, or the means of revealing and expressing his inner life. I try to place myself in the heart of the mystery of this natural rustic life – I, who am civilised, who cannot enjoy by instinct alone, and who am always tormented by the desire of giving an account of my contemplation, or of my meditation, to myself and to others.

'Then, too,' continued my friend, 'I am trying to find out what relation can be established between my intelligence, which is too active, and that of the peasant, which is not active enough; just as I was considering a moment ago what painting, music, description, the interpretation of art, in short, could add to the beauty of the autumnal night which is revealed to me in its mysterious silence, and affects me in some magical and unknown way.'

'Let us see,' said I, 'how your question is put. This October night, this colourless sky, this music without any distinct or connected melody, this calm of nature, and the peasant who by his very simplicity is more able than we to enjoy and understand it, though he cannot portray it – let us put all this together and call it *primitive life*, with relation to our own highly developed and complicated life, which I shall call *artificial life*. You are asking what possible connection or direct link can there be between these two opposite conditions in the existence of persons and things; between the palace and the cottage, between the artist and the universe, between the poet and the labourer.'

'Yes,' he answered, 'and let us be exact: between the language spoken by nature, primitive life, and instinct, and that spoken by art, science – in a word, by *knowledge*.'

'To answer in the language you have adopted, I should say that the link between *knowledge* and sensation is *feeling*.'

'It is about the definition of feeling that I am going to question you and myself, for its mission is the interpretation which is troubling me. It is the art or artist, if you prefer, empowered to translate the purity, grace and charm of the primitive life to those who only live the artificial life, and who are, if you will allow me to say so, the greatest fools in the world in the presence of nature and her divine secrets.'

'You are asking nothing less than the secret of art, and you must look for it in the breast of God. No artist can reveal it, for he does not know it himself, and cannot give an account of the sources of his own inspiration or his own weakness. How shall one attempt to express beauty, simplicity and truth? Do I know? And can anybody teach us? No, not even the greatest artists, because if they tried to do so they would cease to be artists, and would become critics; and criticism—'

13

'And criticism,' rejoined my friend, 'has been revolving for centuries about the mystery without understanding it. But, excuse me, that is not exactly what I meant. I am still more radical at this moment, and call the power of art in question. I despise it, I annihilate it, I declare that art is not born, that it does not exist; or, if it has been, its time is past. It is exhausted, it has no more expression, no more breath of life, no more means to sing of the beauty of truth. Nature is a work of art, but God is the only artist that exists, and man is but an arranger in bad taste. Nature is beautiful, and breathes feeling from all her pores; love, youth, beauty are in her imperishable. But man has but foolish means and miserable faculties for feeling and expressing them. He had better keep aloof, silent and absorbed in contemplation. Come, what have you to say?'

'I agree, and am quite satisfied with your opinion,' I answered.

'Ah!' he cried, 'you are going too far, and embrace my paradox too warmly. I am only pleading, and want you to reply.'

'I reply, then, that a sonnet of Petrarch has its relative beauty, which is equivalent to the beauty of the water of Vaucluse; that a fine landscape of Ruysdael has a charm which equals that of this evening; that Mozart sings in the language of men as well as Philomel in that of birds;* that Shakespeare delineates passions, emotions, and instincts as vividly as the actual primitive man can experience them. This is art and its relativeness – in short, feeling.'

'Yes, it is all a work of transformation! But suppose that it does not satisfy me? Even if you were a thousand times in the right according to the decrees of taste and aesthetics, what if I think Petrarch's verses less harmonious than the roar of the waterfall, and so on? If I maintain that there is in this evening a charm that no one could reveal to me unless I had felt it myself; and that all Shakespeare's passion is cold in comparison with that I see gleaming in the eyes of a jealous peasant who beats his wife, what should you have to say? You must convince my feeling. And if it eludes your examples and resists your proofs? Art is not an invincible demonstrator, and feeling not always satisfied by the best definition.'

'I have really nothing to answer except that art is a demonstration of which nature is the proof; that the pre-existing fact of the proof is always present to justify or contradict the demonstration, which nobody can make successfully unless he examine the proof with religious love.'

'So the demonstration could not do without the proof; but could the proof do without the demonstration?'

'No doubt God could do without it; but, although you are talking as if you did not belong to us, I am willing to wager that you would understand nothing of the proof if you had not found the demonstration under a thousand forms in the tradition of art, and if you were not yourself a demonstration constantly acting upon the proof.'

'That is just what I am complaining of. I should like to rid myself of this eternal irritating demonstration; to erase from my memory the teachings and the forms of art; never to think of painting when I look at a landscape, of music when I listen to the wind, or of poetry when I admire and take delight in both together. I should like to enjoy everything instinctively, because I think that the cricket which is singing just now is more joyous and ecstatic than I.'

'You complain, then, of being a man?'

'No; I complain of being no longer a primitive man.'

'It remains to be known whether he was capable of enjoying what he could not understand.'

'I do not suppose that he was similar to the brutes, for as soon as he became a man he thought and felt differently from them. But I cannot form an exact idea of his emotions, and that is what bothers me. I should like to be what the existing state of society allows a great number of men to be from the cradle to the grave – I should like to be a peasant; a peasant who does not know how to read, whom God has endowed with good instincts, a serene organisation and an upright conscience; and I fancy that in the sluggishness of my useless faculties, and in the ignorance of depraved tastes, I should be as happy as the primitive man of Jean-Jacques's dreams.'*

'I, too, have had this same dream; who has not? But, even so, your reasoning is not conclusive, for the most simple and ingenuous peasant may still be an artist; and I believe even that his art is superior to ours. The form is different, but it appeals more strongly to me than all the forms which belong to civilisation. Songs, ballads and rustic tales say in a few words what our literature can only amplify and disguise.'

'I may triumph, then?' resumed my friend. 'The peasant's art is the best, because it is more directly inspired by nature by being in closer contact with her. I confess I went to extremes in saying that art was good for nothing; but I meant that I should like to feel after the fashion of the peasant, and I do not contradict myself now. There are certain Breton laments, made by beggars, which in three couplets are worth all Goethe and Byron put together, and which prove that appreciation of truth and beauty was more spontaneous and complete in such simple souls than in our most distinguished poets. And music, too! Is not our country full of lovely melodies? And though they do not possess painting as an art, they have it in their speech, which is a hundred times more expressive, forcible and logical than our literary language.'

'I agree with you,' said I, 'especially as to this last point. It drives me to despair that I am obliged to write in the language of the Academy,* when I am much more familiar with another tongue infinitely more fitted for expressing a whole order of emotions, thoughts and feelings.'

'Oh, yes!' said he, 'that fresh and unknown world is closed to modern art, and no study can help you to express it even to yourself, with all your sympathies for the peasant, if you try to introduce it into the domain of civilised art and the intellectual intercourse of artificial life.'

'Alas!' I answered, 'this thought has often disturbed me. I have myself seen and felt, in common with all civilised beings, that primitive life was the dream and ideal of all men and all times. From the shepherds of Longus down to those of Trianon,* pastoral life has been a perfumed Eden, where souls wearied and harassed by the tumult of the world have sought a refuge. Art, which has always flattered and fawned upon the too fortunate among mankind, has passed through an unbroken series of pastorals. And under the title of *The History of Pastorals* I have often wished to write a learned and critical work, in which to review all the different rural dreams to which the upper classes have so fondly clung.

'I should follow their modifications, which are always in inverse relation to the depravity of morals, for they become innocent and sentimental in proportion as society is shameless and corrupt. I should like to *order* this book of a writer better qualified than I to accomplish it, and then I should read it with delight. It should be a complete treatise on art; for music, painting, architecture, literature in all its forms, the theatre, poetry, romances, eclogues, songs, fashions, gardens, and even dress, have been influenced by the infatuation for the pastoral dream. All the types of the golden age, the shepherdesses of Astraea,* who are first nymphs and then marchionesses, and who pass through the Lignon of Florian,* wear satin and powder under Louis XV, and are put into sabots* by Sedaine* at the end of the monarchy, are all more or less false, and seem to us today contemptible and ridiculous. We have done with them, and see only their ghosts at the opera; and yet they once reigned at court and were the delight of kings, who borrowed from them the shepherd's crook and scrip.

'I have often wondered why there are no more shepherds, for we are not so much in love with the truth lately that art and literature can afford to despise the old conventional types rather than those introduced by the present mode. Today we are devoted to force and brutality, and on the background of these passions we embroider decorations horrible enough to make our hair stand on end if we could take them seriously.'

'If we have no more shepherds,' rejoined my friend, 'and if literature has changed one false ideal for another, is it not an involuntary attempt of art to bring itself down to the level of the intelligence of all classes? Does not the dream of equality afloat in society impel art to a fierce brutality in order to awaken those instincts and passions common to all men, of whatever rank they may be? Nobody has as yet reached the truth. It exists no more in a hideous realism than in an embellished idealism; but there is plainly a search for it, and if the search is in the wrong direction, the eagerness of the pursuit is only quickened. Let us see: the drama, poetry and the novel have thrown away the shepherd's crook for the dagger, and when rustic life appears on the scene it has a stamp of reality which was wanting in the old pastorals. But there is no more poetry in it, I am sorry to say; and I do not yet see the means of reinstating the pastoral ideal without making it either too gaudy or too sombre. You have often thought of doing it, I know; but can you hope for success?'

'No,' I answered, 'for there is no form for me to adopt, and there is no language in which to express my conception of rustic simplicity. If I made the labourer of the fields speak as he does speak, it would be necessary to have a translation on the opposite page for the civilised reader; and if I made him speak as we do, I should create an impossible being, in whom it would be necessary to suppose an order of ideas which he does not possess.'

'Even if you made him speak as he does speak, your own language would constantly make a disagreeable contrast; and in my opinion you cannot escape this criticism. You describe a peasant girl, call her *Jeanne*, and put into her mouth words which she might possibly use. But you, who are the writer of the novel, and are anxious to make your readers understand your fondness for painting this kind of type – you compare her to a druidess, to a Jeanne d'Arc, and so on. Your opinions and language make an incongruous effect with hers, like the clashing of harsh colours in a picture; and this is not the way fully to enter into nature, even if you idealise her. Since then you have made a better and more truthful study in *The Devil's Pool*.* Still, I am not yet satisfied; the tip of the author's finger is apparent from time to time; and there are some author's words, as they are called by Henri Meunier,* an artist who has succeeded in being true in caricature, and who has consequently solved the problem he had set for himself. I know that your own problem is no easier to solve. But you must still try, although you are sure of not succeeding; masterpieces are only lucky attempts. You may console yourself for not achieving masterpieces, provided that your attempts are conscientious.'

'I am consoled beforehand,' I answered, 'and I am willing to begin again whenever you wish; please give me your advice.'

'For example,' said he, 'we were present last evening at a rustic gathering at the farm, and the hemp-dresser told a story until two o'clock in the morning. The priest's servant helped him with his tale, and resumed it when he stopped; she was a peasant woman of some slight education; he was uneducated, but happily gifted by nature and endowed with a certain rude eloquence. Between them they related a true story, which was rather long, and like a simple kind of novel. Can you remember it?'

'Perfectly, and I could repeat it word for word in their language.'

'But their language would require a translation; you must write in your own, without using a single word unintelligible enough to necessitate a footnote for the reader.'

'I see that you are setting an impossible task for me – a task into which I have never plunged without emerging dissatisfied with myself, and overcome with a sense of my own weakness.'

'No matter, you must plunge in again, for I understand you artists; you need obstacles to rouse your enthusiasm, and you never do well what is plain and easy to you. Come, begin, tell me the story of the "Waif", but not in the way that you and I heard it last night. That was a masterly piece of narrative for you and me who are children of the soil. But tell it to me as if you had on your right hand a Parisian speaking the modern tongue, and on your left a peasant before whom you were unwilling to utter a word or phrase which he could not understand. You must speak dearly for the Parisian, and simply for the peasant. One will accuse you of a lack of local colour, and the other of a lack of elegance. But I shall be listening too, and I am trying to discover by what means art, without ceasing to be universal, can penetrate the mystery of primitive simplicity, and interpret the charm of nature to the mind.'

'This, then, is a study which we are going to undertake together?'

'Yes, for I shall interrupt you when you stumble.'

'Very well, let us sit down on this bank covered with wild thyme. I will begin; but first allow me to clear my voice with a few scales.'

'What do you mean? I did not know that you could sing.'

'I am only speaking metaphorically. Before beginning a work of art, I think it is well to call to mind some theme or other to serve as a type, and to induce the desired frame of mind. So, in order to prepare myself for what you ask, I must recite the story of the dog of Brisquet,* which is short, and which I know by heart.'

'What is it? I cannot recall it.'

'It is an exercise for my voice, written by Charles Nodier, who tried his in all possible keys; a great artist, to my thinking, and one who has never received all the applause he deserved, because, among all his varied attempts, he failed more often than he succeeded. But when a man has achieved two or three masterpieces, no matter how short they may be, he should be crowned, and his mistakes should be forgotten. Here is the dog of Brisquet. You must listen.'

Then I repeated to my friend the story of the Bichonne, which moved him to tears, and which he declared to be a masterpiece of style.

'I should be discouraged in what I am going to attempt,' said I, 'for this odyssey of the poor dog of Brisquet, which did not take five minutes to recite, has no stain or blot; it is a diamond cut by the first lapidary in the world – for Nodier is essentially a lapidary in literature. I am not scientific, and must call sentiment to my aid. Then, too, I cannot promise to be brief, for I know beforehand that my study will fail in the first of all requisites, that of being short and good at the same time.'

'Go on, nevertheless,' said my friend, bored by my preliminaries.

'This, then, is the history of *François the Champi*,' I resumed, 'and I shall try to remember the first part without any alteration. It was Monique, the old servant of the priest, who began.'

'One moment,' said my severe auditor, 'I must object to your title. *Champi* is not French.'

'I beg your pardon,' I answered. 'The dictionary says it is obsolete, but Montaigne* uses it, and I do not wish to be more French than the great writers who have created the language. So I shall not call my story *François the Foundling*, nor *François the Bastard*, but *François the Champi* – that is to say, the Waif, the forsaken child of the fields, as he was once called in the great world, and is still called in our part of the country.'

CHAPTER I

O NE MORNING, when Madeleine Blanchet, the young wife of the miller of Cormouer, went down to the end of her meadow to wash her linen in the fountain, she found a little child sitting in front of her washing-board playing with the straw she used as a cushion for her knees. Madeleine Blanchet looked at the child, and was surprised not to recognise him, for the road which runs nearby is unfrequented, and few strangers are to be met with in the neighbourhood.

'Who are you, my boy?' said she to the little boy, who turned confidingly towards her, but did not seem to understand her question. 'What is your name?' Madeleine Blanchet went on, as she made him sit down beside her, and knelt down to begin to wash.

'François,' answered the child.

'François who?'

'Who?' said the child stupidly.

'Whose son are you?'

'I don't know.'

'You don't know your father's name?'

'I have no father.'

'Is he dead then?'

'I don't know.'

'And your mother?'

'She is over there,' said the child, pointing to a poor little hovel which stood at the distance of two gunshots from the mill, and the thatched roof of which could be seen through the willows.

'Oh! I know,' said Madeleine. 'Is she the woman who has come to live here, and who moved in last evening?'

'Yes,' answered the child.

'And you used to live at Mers?'

'I don't know.'

'You are not a wise child. Do you know your mother's name, at least?'

'Yes, it is Zabelle.'

'Isabelle who? Don't you know her other name?'

'No, of course not.'

'What you know will not wear your brains out,' said Madeleine, smiling and beginning to beat her linen.

'What do you say?' asked little François. Madeleine looked at him again; he was a fine child, and had magnificent eyes. 'It is a pity,' she thought, 'that he seems to be so idiotic. How old are you?' she continued. 'Perhaps you do not know that either.'

The truth is that he knew no more about this than about the rest. He tried his best to answer, ashamed to have the miller's wife think him so foolish, and delivered himself of this brilliant reply:

'Two years old.'

'Indeed?' said Madeleine, wringing out her linen, without looking at him any more, 'you are a real little simpleton, and nobody has taken the trouble to teach you, my poor child.

You are tall enough to be six years old, but you have not the sense of a child of two.'

'Perhaps,' answered François. Then, making another effort, as if to shake off the lethargy from his poor little mind, he said: 'Were you asking for my name? It is François the Waif.'

'Oh! I understand now,' said Madeleine, looking at him compassionately; and she was no longer astonished that he was so dirty, ragged and stupid.

'You have not clothes enough,' said she, 'and the weather is chill; I am sure that you must be cold.'

'I do not know,' answered the poor waif, who was so accustomed to suffering that he was no longer conscious of it.

Madeleine sighed. She thought of her little Jeannie, who was only a year old, and was sleeping comfortably in his cradle watched over by his grandmother, while this poor little waif was shivering all alone at the fountain's brink, preserved from drowning only by the mercy of Providence, for he was too foolish to know that he would die if he fell into the water.

Madeleine, whose heart was full of kindness, felt the child's arm and found it warm, although he shook from time to time, and his pretty face was very pale.

'Have you any fever?' she asked.

'I don't know,' answered the child, who was always feverish.

Madeleine Blanchet loosened the woollen shawl from her shoulders and wrapped it round the waif, who let her have her way without showing either surprise or pleasure. She picked up all the straw from under his knees and made a bed for him, on which he soon fell asleep; then she made haste to finish washing her little Jeannie's clothes, for she nursed her baby and was anxious to return to him.

When her task was completed, the wet linen was twice as heavy as before, and she could not carry it all. She took home what she could, and left the rest with her wooden beater beside the water, intending to come back immediately and wake up the waif. Madeleine Blanchet was neither tall nor strong. She was a very pretty woman, with a fearless spirit and a reputation for sense and sweetness.

As she opened the door of her house she heard the clattering of sabots running after her over the little bridge above the mill-dam, and, turning round, she saw the waif, who had caught up with her, and was bringing her her beater, her soap, the rest of the linen and her shawl.

'Oh!' said she, laying her hand on his shoulder. 'You are not so foolish as I thought, for you are obliging, and nobody who has a good heart can be stupid. Come in, my child, come in and rest. Look at this poor little boy! He is carrying a load heavier than himself! Here,' said she to the miller's old mother, who handed her her baby, rosy and smiling, 'here is a poor sick-looking waif. You understand fevers, and we must try to cure him.'

'Ah! That is the fever of poverty!' replied the old woman, as she looked at François. 'He could cure it with good soup, but he cannot get that. He is the little waif that belongs to the woman who moved in yesterday. She is your husband's tenant, Madeleine. She looks very wretched, and I am afraid that she will not pay regularly.'

Madeleine did not answer. She knew that her husband and her mother-in-law were not charitable, and that they loved their money more than their neighbour. She nursed her baby, and when the old woman had gone out to drive home the geese she took François by the hand, and, holding Jeannie on her arm, went with them to Zabelle's.

Zabelle, whose real name was Isabelle Bigot, was an old maid of fifty, as disinterested as a woman can be when she has nothing to live on, and is in constant dread of starvation. She had taken François after he was weaned, from a dying woman, and had brought him up ever since, for the sake of the monthly payment of a few pieces of silver, and with the expectation of making a little servant out of him. She had lost her sheep, and was forced to buy others on credit, whenever she could obtain it; for she had no other means of support than her little flock, and a dozen hens, which lived at the expense of the parish. She meant François to tend this poor flock along the roadsides, until he should be old enough to make his first communion, after which she expected to hire him out as best she could, either as a little swineherd or a ploughboy, and she was sure that if his heart were good he would give part of his wages to his adopted mother.

Zabelle had come from Mers, the day after the feast of St Martin, leaving her last goat behind her in payment of what she owed on her rent, and had taken possession of the little cottage belonging to the mill of Cormouer, without being able to offer any security beside her pallet bed, two chairs, a chest and a few earthen vessels. The house was so poor, so ill-protected from the weather and of such trifling value, that the miller was obliged to incur the risk of letting it to a poor tenant, or to leave it unoccupied.

Madeleine talked with Zabelle, and soon perceived that she was not a bad woman, and that she would do all in her power to pay the rent. She had some affection for the waif, but she was so accustomed to see him suffer and to suffer herself that she was at first more surprised than pleased by the pity which the rich miller's wife showed for the forlorn child.

At last, after she had recovered from her astonishment, and understood that Madeleine had not come to ask anything of her, but to do her a kindness, she took courage, related her story, which was like that of all the unfortunate, and thanked her warmly for her interest. Madeleine assured her that she would do her best to help her, but begged her to tell nobody, acknowledging that she was not her own mistress at home, and could only afford her assistance in secret.

She left her woollen shawl with Zabelle, and exacted a promise from her that she would cut it into a coat for the waif that same evening, and not allow the pieces to be seen before they were sewed together. She saw, indeed, that Zabelle consented reluctantly, thinking the shawl very convenient for her own use, and so she was obliged to tell her that she would do no more for her unless the waif were warmly clothed in three days' time.

'Do you not suppose,' she added, 'that my mother-in-law, who is so wide awake, would recognise my shawl on your shoulders? Do you wish to get me into trouble? You may count upon my helping you in other ways if you keep your own counsel. Now, listen to me: your waif has the fever, and he will die if you do not take good care of him.'

'Do you think so?' said Zabelle. 'I should be very sorry to lose him, because he has the best heart in the world; he never complains, and is as obedient as if he belonged to a respectable family. He is quite different from other waifs, who are ill-tempered and unruly, and always in mischief.'

'That is only because they are rebuffed and ill-treated. If yours is good, it is because you have been kind to him, you may be sure.'

'That is true,' rejoined Zabelle; 'children are more grateful than people think, and though this little fellow is not bright, he can be very useful at times. Once, when I was ill last year, and he was only five years old, he took as good care of me as if he were a grown-up person.'

'Listen,' said the miller's wife: 'you must send him to me every morning and evening, at the hour when I give soup to my child. I shall make more than is necessary, and the waif may eat what is left; nobody will pay any attention.'

'Oh! I shall not dare bring him to you, and he will never have enough sense to know the right time himself.'

'Let us arrange it in this way. When the soup is ready, I will put my distaff on the bridge over the dam. Look, you can see it very well from here. Then you must send the child over with a sabot in his hand, as if he were coming to get a light for the fire; and if he eats my soup, you will have all yours to yourself. You will both be better fed.'

'That will do very well,' answered Zabelle. 'I see that you are a clever woman, and that I am fortunate in coming here. I was very much afraid of your husband, who has the reputation of being a hard man, and if I could have gone elsewhere I should not have taken his house, especially as it is in wretched repair, and the rent is high. But I see that you are kind to the poor, and will help me to bring up my waif. Ah! If the soup could only cure his fever! It would be a great misfortune to me to lose that child! He brings me but little profit, for all that I receive from the asylum goes for his support. But I love him as if he were my own child, because I know that he is good, and will be of use to me later. Have you noticed how well-grown he is for his age, and will soon be able to work?'

Thus François the Waif was reared by the care and kindness of Madeleine, the miller's wife. He soon recovered his health, for he was strongly built, and any rich man in the country might have wished for a son with as handsome a face and as well-knit a frame. He was as brave as a man, and swam in the river like a fish, diving even under the mill-dam; he feared neither fire nor water; he jumped on the wildest colts and rode them without a halter into the pasture, kicking them with his heels to keep them in the right path, and holding on to their manes when they leaped the ditches. It was singular that he did all this in his quiet, easy way, without saying anything or changing his childlike and somewhat sleepy expression.

It was on account of this expression that he passed for a fool; but it is none the less true that if it were a question of robbing a magpie's nest at the top of a lofty poplar, or of finding a cow that had strayed far from home, or of killing a thrush with a stone, no child was bolder, more adroit or more certain of success than he. The other children called it *luck*, which is supposed to be the portion of a waif in this hard world. So they always let him take the first part in dangerous amusements.

'He will never get hurt,' they said, 'because he is a waif. A kernel of wheat fears the havoc of the storm, but a random seed never dies.'

For two years all went well. Zabelle found means to buy a few sheep and goats, though no one knew how. She rendered a good many small services to the mill, and Cadet Blanchet, the miller, was induced to make some repairs in her roof, which leaked in every direction. She was enabled to dress herself and her waif a little better, and looked gradually less poverty-stricken than on her arrival. Madeleine's mother-in-law made some harsh comments on the disappearance of certain articles, and on the quantity of bread consumed in the house, and once Madeleine was obliged to plead guilty in order to shield Zabelle from suspicion; but, contrary to his mother's expectation, Cadet Blanchet was hardly angry at all, and seemed to wink at what his wife had done.

The secret of Cadet Blanchet's compliance was that he was still very much in love with his wife. Madeleine was pretty, and not the least of a coquette; he heard her praises sung everywhere. Besides, his affairs were prosperous, and, as he was one of those men who are cruel only when they are in dread of calamity, he was kinder to Madeleine than anybody could have supposed possible. This roused Mother Blanchet's jealousy, and she revenged herself by petty annoyances, which Madeleine bore in silence, and without complaining to her husband.

It was the best way of putting an end to them, and no woman could be more patient and reasonable in this respect than Madeleine. But they say in our country that goodness avails less in the end than malice, and the day came when Madeleine was rebuked and called to account for her charities.

It was a year when the grain had been wasted by hail, and an overflow of the river had spoiled the hay. Cadet Blanchet was not in a good humour, and one day, as he was coming back from market with a comrade who had just married a very beautiful girl, the latter said to him:

'You, too, were not to be pitied *in your day*, for your Madelon used to be a very attractive girl.'

'What do you mean by *my day*, and *Madelon used to be*? Do you think that she and I are old? Madeleine is not twenty yet, and I am not aware that she has lost her looks.'

'Oh, no, I do not say so,' replied the other. 'Madeleine is certainly still good-looking; but you know that when a woman marries so young you cannot expect her to be pretty long. After she has nursed one child, she is already worn; and your wife was never strong, for you see that she is very thin, and has lost the appearance of health. Is the poor thing ill?'

'Not that I know of. Why do you ask me?'

'Oh, I don't know. I think she looks sad, as if she suffered or had some sorrow. A woman's bloom lasts no longer than the blossom of the vine. I must expect to see my wife with a long face and sober expression. And we men are only in love with our wives while we are jealous of them. They exasperate us; we scold them and beat them sometimes; they are distressed and weep; they stay at home and are afraid of us; then they are bored and care no more about us. But we are happy, for we are the masters. And yet, one fine morning, lo and behold, a man sees that if nobody wants his wife, it is because she has grown ugly; so he loves her no longer, and goes to court his neighbour's. It is his fate. Good evening, Cadet Blanchet; you kissed my wife rather too warmly tonight; I took note of it, though I said nothing. I tell you this to let you know that she and I shall not quarrel over it, and that I shall try not to make her as melancholy as yours, because I know my own character. If I am ever jealous, I shall be cruel, and when I have no more occasion for jealousy I shall be still worse, perhaps.'

A good disposition profits by a good lesson; but, though active and intelligent, Cadet Blanchet was too arrogant to keep his self-possession. He came home with his head high and his eye bloodshot. He looked at Madeleine as he had not done for a long time, and perceived that she was pale and altered. He asked her if she were ill, so rudely that she turned still paler, and answered in a faint voice that she was quite well. He took offence, Heaven knows why, and sat down to the table, desirous of seeking a quarrel. He had not long to wait for an opportunity. They talked of the dearness of wheat, and Mother Blanchet remarked, as she did every evening, that too much bread was eaten in the house. Madeleine was silent. Cadet Blanchet wanted to make her responsible for the waste, and the old woman declared that she had caught the waif carrying away half a loaf that very morning. Madeleine should have been indignant and held her own, but she could only cry. Blanchet thought of what his companion had said to him, and was still more irritated; and so it happened that from that day on, explain it as you can, he no longer loved his wife, but made her wretched.

CHAPTER II

HE MADE HER WRETCHED, and as he had never made her happy she was doubly unlucky in her marriage. She had allowed herself to be married, at sixteen, to this rough, red-faced man, who drank deeply on Sunday, was in a fury all Monday, in bad spirits on Tuesday, and worked like a horse all the rest of the week to make up for lost time, for he was avaricious, and had no leisure to think of his wife. He was less ill-tempered on Saturday, because he had finished his work, and expected to amuse himself next day. But a single day of good humour in a week is not enough, and Madeleine had no pleasure in seeing him merry, because she knew that he would be sure to come home the next evening in a passion.

But as she was young and pretty, and so gentle that it was impossible to be angry long with her, there were still intervals when he was kind and just, and when he took her hands in his and said:

'Madeleine, you are a good wife, and I think that you were made expressly for me. If I had married a coquette, such as so many women are, I should kill her, or I should drown myself under my own mill wheel. But I know that you are well-behaved and industrious, and that you are worth your weight in gold.'

After four years of married life, however, his love had quite gone; he had no more kind words for her, and was enraged that she made no answer to his abuse. What answer could she make? She knew that her husband was unjust, and was unwilling to reproach him for it, for she considered it her duty to respect the master whom she had never been able to love.

Mother Blanchet was pleased to see her son master of the house again, as she said; just as if it had ever been otherwise. She hated her daughter-in-law, because she knew her to be better than herself. When she could find no other cause of complaint, she reviled her for not being strong, for coughing all winter and for having only one child. She despised her for this, for knowing how to read and write, and for reading prayers in a corner of the orchard, instead of gossiping and chattering with the dames of the vicinity.

Madeleine placed her soul in God's hands, and, thinking lamentations useless, she bore her affliction as if it were her due. She withdrew her heart from this earth, and often dreamed of paradise, as if she wished to die. Still, she was careful of her health, and armed herself with courage, because she knew that her child could only be happy through her, and she accepted everything for the sake of the love she bore him.

Though she could not feel any great affection for Zabelle, she was still fond of her, because this woman, who was half good and half selfish, continued to do her best for the poor waif; and Madeleine, who saw how people deteriorate who think of themselves alone, was inclined to esteem only those who thought sometimes of others. As she was the only person in the neighbourhood who took no care of herself, she was entirely isolated and very sorrowful, without fully understanding the cause of her grief.

Little by little, however, she observed that the waif, who was then ten years old, began to think as she did. When I say think, I mean you to understand that she judged from his behaviour; for there was no more sense in the poor child's words than on the first day she had spoken with him. He could not express himself, and when people tried to make him talk they were sure to interrupt him immediately, for he knew nothing about anything. But if he were needed to run an errand, he was always ready, and when it was an errand for Madeleine, he ran before she could ask him. He looked as if he had not understood the commission, but he executed it so swiftly and well that even she was amazed.

One day, as he was carrying little Jeannie in his arms, and allowing him to pull his hair for his amusement, Madeleine caught the child from him with some slight irritation, saying half involuntarily:

'François, if you begin now by suffering all the whims of other people, there is no knowing where they will stop.'

To her great surprise, François answered:

'I should rather suffer evil than return it.'

Madeleine was astonished, and gazed into the eyes of the waif, where she saw something she had never observed in the eyes even of the most honest persons she knew; something so kind, and yet so decided, that she was quite bewildered. She sat down on the grass with her child on her knees, and made the waif sit on the edge of her dress, without daring to speak to him. She could scarcely understand why she was overcome with fear and shame that she had often jested with this child for being so foolish. It is true that she had always done so with extreme gentleness, and perhaps she had pitied and loved him the more for his stupidity; but now she fancied that he had always understood her ridicule, and had been pained by it without being able to say anything in return.

She soon forgot this incident; for a short time afterwards her husband, who had become infatuated with a disreputable woman in the neighbourhood, undertook to hate his wife in good earnest, and to forbid her to allow Zabelle and her boy to enter the mill. Madeleine fell to thinking of still more secret means of aiding them, and warned Zabelle, telling her that she should pretend to neglect her for a time.

Zabelle was very much in awe of the miller, and had not Madeleine's power of endurance for the love of others. She argued to herself that the miller was the master, and could turn her out of doors, or increase her rent, and that Madeleine would be unable to prevent it. She reflected also that if she submitted to Mother Blanchet, she would establish herself in the good graces of the old woman, whose protection would be more useful to her than that of the young wife. So she went to the miller's mother, and confessed that she had received help from her daughter-in-law, declaring that she had done so against her will, and only out of pity for the waif, whom she had no means of feeding. The old woman detested the waif, though for no reason except that Madeleine took an interest in him. She advised Zabelle to rid herself of him, and promised her at this price to obtain six months' credit on her rent. The morrow of St Martin's day had come round, and as the year had been a hard one, Zabelle was out of money, and Madeleine was so closely watched that for some time she had been unable to give her any. Zabelle boldly promised to take back the waif to the foundling asylum the next day.

She had no sooner given her word than she repented of it, and at the sight of little François sleeping on his wretched pallet, her heart was as heavy as if she were about to commit a mortal sin. She could not sleep, and before dawn Mother Blanchet entered the hovel.

'Come, get up, Zabeau,' she said. 'You gave me your promise and you must keep it. If you wait to speak to my daughter-in-law, you will never do anything, but you must let the boy go, in her interest as well as your own, you see. My son has taken a dislike to him on account of his stupidity and greediness; my daughter-in-law has pampered him too much, and I am sure that he is a thief already. All foundlings are thieves from their birth, and it is mere folly to expect anything of such brats. This one will be the cause of your being driven away from here, and will ruin your reputation; he will furnish my son with a reason for beating his wife every day, and in the end, when he is tall and strong, he will become a highwayman, and will bring you to shame. Come, come, you must start! Take him through the fields as far as Corley, and there the stagecoach passes at eight o'clock. Get in with him, and you will reach Châteauroux, at noon, at the latest. You can come back this evening; there is a piece of money for your journey, and you will have enough left over to amuse yourself with in town.'

Zabelle woke the child, dressed him in his best, made a bundle of the rest of his clothes, and, taking his hand, started off with him by the light of the moon.

As she walked along and the day broke, her heart failed her; she could neither hasten her steps nor speak, and when she came to the high road, she sat down on the side of a ditch, more dead than alive. The stagecoach was approaching, and they had arrived only just in time.

The waif was not in the habit of worrying, and thus far he had followed his mother without suspicion; but when he saw a huge carriage bowling towards him for the first time in his life, the noise it made frightened him, and he tried to pull Zabelle back into the meadow which they had just left to join the high road. Zabelle thought that he understood his fate, and said:

'Come, poor François, you really must!'

François was still more frightened. He thought that the stagecoach was an enormous animal running after him to devour him. He who was so bold in meeting all the dangers which he knew lost his head, and rushed back screaming into the meadow. Zabelle ran after him; but when she saw him pale as death, her courage deserted her. She followed him all across the meadow, and allowed the stagecoach to go by.

CHAPTER III

THEY RETURNED BY the same road they had come, until they had gone half the distance, and then they stopped to rest. Zabelle was alarmed to see that the child trembled from head to foot, and his heart beat so violently as to agitate his poor old shirt. She made him sit down, and attempted to comfort him, but she did not know what she was saying, and François was not in a state to guess her meaning. She drew out a bit of bread from her basket and tried to persuade him to eat it; but he had no desire for food, and they sat on for a long time in silence.

At last, Zabelle, who was in the habit of recurring to her first thoughts, was ashamed of her weakness, and said to herself that she would be lost if she appeared again at the mill with the child. Another stage was to pass towards noon, and she decided to stay where they were until the moment necessary for returning to the high road; but as François was so terrified that he had lost the little sense he possessed, and as for the first time in his life he was capable of resisting her will, she tried to tempt him with the attractions of the horse's bells, the noise of the wheels, and the speed of the great vehicle.

In her efforts to inspire him with confidence, she said more than she intended; perhaps her repentance urged her to speak, in spite of herself, or it may be that when François woke that morning he had heard certain words of Mother Blanchet, which now returned to his mind; or else his poor wits cleared suddenly at the approach of calamity; at all events, he began to say, with the same expression in his eyes which had once astonished and almost startled Madeleine:

'Mother, you want to send me away from you! You want to take me far off from here and leave me.'

Then he remembered the word asylum, spoken several times in his hearing. He had no idea what an asylum was, but it seemed to him more horrible than the stagecoach, and he cried with a shudder:

'You want to put me in the asylum!'

Zabelle had gone too far to retreat. She believed that the child knew more of her intentions than he really did, and without reflecting how easy it would be to deceive him and rid herself of him by stratagem, she undertook to explain the truth to him, and to make him understand that he would be much happier at the asylum than with her, that he would be better cared for there, would learn to work, and would be placed for a time in the charge of some woman less poor than herself, who would be a mother to him.

This attempted consolation put the finishing touch to the waif's despair. A strange and unknown future inspired him with more terror than all Zabelle could say of the hardships of a life with her. Besides, he loved with all his might this ungrateful mother, who cared less for him than for herself. He loved another, too, almost as much as Zabelle, and she was Madeleine; only he did not know that he loved her, and did not speak of her. He threw himself sobbing on the ground, tore up the grass with his hands and flung it over his face, as if he had fallen in mortal agony. When Zabelle, in her distress and impatience, tried to make him get up by force and threats, he beat his head so hard against the stones that he was covered with blood, and she thought he was about to kill himself.

It pleased God that Madeleine Blanchet should pass by at that moment. She had heard nothing of the departure of Zabelle and the child, and was coming home from Presles, where she had carried back some wool to a lady, who had given it to her to spin very fine, as she was considered the best spinster far and wide. She had received her payment, and was returning to the mill with ten crowns in her pocket. She was going to cross the river on one of those little plank bridges on a level with the surface of the water, which are often to be met with in that part of the country, when she heard heart-piercing shrieks, and recognised at once the voice of the poor waif. She flew in the direction of the cries, and saw the child, bathed in blood, struggling in Zabelle's arms. She could not understand it at first; for it looked as if Zabelle had cruelly struck him, and were trying to shake him off. This seemed the more probable, as François, on catching sight of her, rushed towards her, twined his arms about her like a little snake, and clung to her skirts, screaming:

'Madame Blanchet, Madame Blanchet, save me!'

Zabelle was tall and strong, and Madeleine was small and slight as a reed. Still, she was not afraid, and, imagining that Zabelle had gone crazy, and was going to murder the child, she placed herself in front of him, resolved to protect him or to die while he was making his escape.

A few words, however, sufficed for an explanation. Zabelle, who was more grieved than angry, told the story, and François, who at last took in all the sadness of his lot, managed this time to profit by what he heard, with more cleverness than he had ever been supposed to possess. After Zabelle had finished, he kept fast hold of the miller's wife, saying:

'Don't send me away, don't let me be sent away.'

And he went to and fro between Zabelle, who was crying, and the miller's wife, who was crying still harder, repeating all kinds of words and prayers, which scarcely seemed to come from his lips, for this was the first time he had ever been able to express himself.

'Oh, my mother, my darling mother!' said he to Zabelle. 'Why do you want me to leave you? Do you want me to die of grief and never see you again? What have I done, that you no longer love me? Have I not always obeyed you? Have I done any harm? I have always taken good care of our animals – you told me so yourself; and when you kissed me every evening, you said I was your child, and you never said that you were not my mother! Keep me, mother, keep me; I am praying to you as I pray to God! I shall always take care of you; I shall always work for you; if you are not satisfied with me, you may beat me, and I shall not mind; but do not send me away until I have done something wrong.'

Then he went to Madeleine, and said:

'Madame Blanchet, take pity on me. Tell my mother to keep me. I shall never go to your house, since it is forbidden, and if you want to give me anything, I shall know that I must not take it. I shall speak to Master Cadet Blanchet, and tell him to beat me and not to scold you on my account. When you go into the fields, I shall always go with you to carry your little boy, and amuse him all day. I shall do all you tell me, and if I do any wrong, you need no longer love me. But do not let me be sent away; I do not want to go; I should rather jump into the river.'

Poor François looked at the river, and ran so near it that they saw his life hung by a thread, and that a single word of refusal would be enough to make him drown himself. Madeleine pleaded for the child, and Zabelle was dying to listen to her. Now that she was near the mill, matters looked differently.

'Well, I will keep you, you naughty child,' said she; 'but I shall be on the road tomorrow, begging my bread because of you. You are too stupid to know it is your fault that I shall be reduced to such a condition, and this is what I have gained by burdening myself with a child who is no good to me, and does not even pay for the bread he eats.'

'You have said enough, Zabelle,' said the miller's wife, taking the child in her arms to lift him from the ground, although he was very heavy. 'There are ten crowns for you to pay your rent with, or to move elsewhere, if my husband persists in driving you away from here. It is my own money – money that I have earned myself. I know that it will be required of me, but no matter. They may kill me if they want; I buy this child, he is mine, he is yours no longer. You do not deserve to keep a child with such a warm heart, and who loves you so much. I shall be his mother, and my family must submit. I am willing to suffer everything for my children. I could be cut in pieces for my Jeannie, and I could endure as much for this child, too. Come, poor François, you are no longer a waif, do you hear? You have a mother, and

44

you can love her as much as you choose, for she will love you with her whole heart in return.'

Madeleine said all this without being perfectly aware of what she was saying. She whose disposition was so gentle was now highly excited. Her heart rebelled against Zabelle, and she was really angry with her. François had thrown his arms round the neck of the miller's wife, and clasped her so tight that she lost her breath; and at the same time her cap and neckerchief were stained with blood, for his head was cut in several places.

Madeleine was so deeply affected, and was filled with so much pity, dismay, sorrow and determination at once that she set out to walk towards the mill with as much courage as a soldier advancing under fire. Without considering that the child was heavy, and she herself so weak that she could hardly carry her small Jeannie, she attempted to cross the unsteady little bridge, which sank under her weight. When she reached the middle, she stopped. The child was so heavy that she swerved slightly, and drops of perspiration started from her forehead. She felt as if she should fall from weakness, when suddenly she called to mind a beautiful and marvellous story that she had read the evening before in an old volume of the *Lives of the Saints*. It was the story of St Christopher, who carried the child Jesus across the river, and found him so heavy that he stopped in fear. She looked down at the waif. His eyes had rolled back in his head, and his arms had relaxed their hold. The poor child had either undergone too much emotion, or he had lost too much blood, and had fainted.

CHAPTER IV

WHEN ZABELLE SAW him thus, she thought he was dead. All her love for him returned, and with no more thought of the miller or his wicked old mother, she seized the child from Madeleine, and began to kiss him, with sobs and cries. They sat down beside the river, and, laying him across their knees, they washed his wounds and staunched the blood with their handkerchiefs; but they had nothing with which to bring him to. Madeleine warmed his head against her bosom, and breathed on his face and into his mouth as people do with the drowned. This revived him, and as soon as he opened his eyes and saw what care they were taking of him, he kissed Madeleine and Zabelle, one after the other, so passionately that they were obliged to check him, fearing that he might faint again.

'Come, come,' said Zabelle, 'we must go home. No, I can never, never leave that child; I see now, and I shall never think of it again. I shall keep your ten crowns, Madeleine, so I can pay my rent tonight if I am forced to do so. Do not tell about it; I shall go tomorrow to the lady in Presles, so that she may not inform against you, and she can say, in case of need, that she has not as yet given you the price of your spinning. In this way we shall gain time, and I shall try so hard that, even if I have to beg for it, I shall succeed in paying my debt to you, so that you need not suffer on my account. You cannot take this child to the mill; your husband would kill him. Leave him to me; I swear to you that I shall take as good care of him as before, and if we are tormented any further, we can think of something else.'

It came to pass that the waif's return was effected without disturbance, and without exciting attention; for it happened that Mother Blanchet had just fallen ill of a stroke of apoplexy, without having had an opportunity of telling her son what she had exacted from Zabelle about the waif, and Master Blanchet sent in all haste for Zabelle to come and help in the household, while Madeleine and the servant were taking care of his mother. For three days everything was in confusion at the mill. Madeleine did not spare herself, and watched for three nights at the bedside of her husband's mother, who died in her arms.

This blow allayed the miller's bad temper for some time. He had loved his mother as much as he was capable of loving, and his vanity was concerned in making as fine a funeral for her as his means allowed. He forgot his mistress for the required time, and with pretended generosity distributed his dead mother's clothes to the poor neighbours. Zabelle had her share of the alms, and the waif received a franc piece, because Blanchet remembered that once, when they were in urgent need of leeches for the sick woman, and everybody was running futilely hither and thither to look for them, the waif went off, without saying a word, to fish some out of a pool where he knew they were, and brought them back in less time than it took the others to start out for them.

So Cadet Blanchet gradually forgot his dislike, and nobody at the mill knew of Zabelle's freak of sending back the waif to the asylum. The question of Madeleine's ten crowns came up later, for the miller did not neglect to make Zabelle pay the rent for her wretched cottage. Madeleine said that she had lost them as she ran home through the fields, on hearing of her mother-in-law's accident. Blanchet made a long search for them and scolded a great deal, but he never found out the use to which the money had been put, and Zabelle was not suspected.

After his mother's death, Blanchet's disposition changed little by little, though not for the better. He found life still more tedious at home, was less observant of what went on, and less niggardly in his expenditure. He no longer earned anything, and, in proportion as he grew fat, led a disorderly life, and cared no more for his work. He looked to make his profit by dishonest bargains and unfair dealings, which would have enriched him, if he had not spent on one hand what he gained on the other. His mistress acquired more ascendency over him every day. She took him with her to fairs and feasts, induced him to engage in petty trickeries, and spend his time at the tavern. He learned how to gamble, and was often lucky; but it would have been better for him to lose always than acquire this unfortunate taste; for his dissipations threw him entirely off his balance, and at the most trifling loss he became furious with himself, and ill-tempered towards everybody else.

While he was leading this wretched life, his wife, always wise and good, governed the house and tenderly reared their only child. But she thought herself doubly a mother, for she loved and watched over the waif almost as much as if he were her own. As her husband became more dissolute, she was less miserable and more her own mistress. In the beginning of his licentious career he was still very churlish, because he dreaded reproaches, and wished to hold his wife in a state of fear and subjection. When he saw that she was by nature an enemy to strife, and showed no jealousy, he made up his mind to leave her in peace. As his mother was no longer there to stir him up against her, he was obliged to recognise that no other woman was as thrifty as Madeleine. He grew accustomed to spend whole weeks away from home, and whenever he came back in the mood for a quarrel, he met with a mute patience that turned away his wrath, and he was first astonished and ended by going to sleep. So finally he came to see his wife only when he was tired and in need of rest.

Madeleine must have been a very Christian woman to live thus alone with an old servant and two children, and perhaps she was a still better Christian than if she had been a nun. God had given her the great privilege of learning to read, and of understanding what she read. Yet she always read the same thing, for she possessed only two books, the Holy Gospel and an abbreviated copy of the *Lives of the Saints*. The Gospel sanctified her, and saddened her to tears, when she read alone in the evening beside her son's bed. The *Lives of the Saints* produced a different effect upon her; it was just as when idle people read stories and excite themselves over dreams and illusions. These beautiful tales inspired her with courage and even gaiety. Sometimes, out in the fields, the waif saw her smile and flush when she had her book in her lap. He wondered at it, and found it hard to understand how the stories which she told him, with some little alteration in order to adapt them to his capacity (and also perhaps because she could not perfectly grasp them from beginning to end), could come from that thing which she called her book. He wanted to read, too, and learned so quickly and well that she was amazed, and in his turn he was able to teach little Jeannie. When François was old enough to make his first communion, Madeleine helped him with his catechism, and the parish priest was delighted with the intelligence and excellent memory of this child, who had always passed for a simpleton, because he was very shy and never had anything to say.

After his first communion, and he was old enough to be hired out, Zabelle was pleased to have him engaged as servant at the mill; and Master Blanchet made no opposition, because it was plain to all that the waif was a good boy, very industrious and obliging, and stronger, more alert and sensible than the other children of his age. Then, too, he was satisfied with ten crowns for wages, and it was an economical arrangement for the miller. François was very happy to be entirely in the service of Madeleine and the dear little Jeannie he loved so much, and when he found that Zabelle could pay for her farm with his earnings, and thus be relieved of her most besetting care, he thought himself as rich as a king.

Unfortunately, poor Zabelle could not long enjoy her reward. At the beginning of the winter, she fell seriously ill, and in spite of receiving every care from the waif and Madeleine, she died on Candlemas Day, after having so far recovered that they thought her well again. Madeleine sorrowed and wept for her sincerely, but she tried to comfort the poor waif, who but for her would have been inconsolable.

Even after a year's time, he still thought of her every day, and almost every instant. Once he said to the miller's wife:

'I feel a kind of remorse when I pray for my poor mother's soul; it is because I did not love her enough. I am very sure that I always did my best to please her, that I never said any but kind words to her, and that I served her in all ways as I serve you; but I must confess something, Madame Blanchet, which troubles me, and for which, in secret, I often ask God's forgiveness. Ever since the day my poor mother wanted to send me back to the asylum, and you took my part, and prevented her doing so, my love for her, against my will, grew less. I was not angry with her; I did not allow myself even to think that she was wrong in trying to rid herself of me. It was her right to do so; I stood in her way; she was afraid of your mother-in-law, and after all she did it very reluctantly; for I could see that she loved me greatly. In some way or other, the idea keeps recurring to my mind, and I cannot drive it away. From the moment you said to me those words which I shall never forget, I loved you more than her, and in spite of all I could do, I thought of you more often than of her. She is dead now, and I did not die of grief as I should if you died!'

'What were the words I said, my poor child, that made you love me so much? I do not remember them.'

'You do not remember them?' said the waif, sitting down at the feet of Madeleine, who was turning her wheel as she listened. 'When you gave the crowns to my mother, you said: "There, I buy that child of you; he is mine!" And then you kissed me and said: "Now you are no longer a waif; you have a mother who will love you as if you were her own!" Did not you say so, Madame Blanchet?'

'If I did, I said what I meant, and am still of the same mind. Do you think I have failed to keep my word?'

'Oh no! Only—'

'Only what?'

'No. I cannot tell you, for it is wrong to complain and be thankless and ungrateful.'

'I know that you cannot be ungrateful, and I want you to say what you have on your mind. Come, in what respect don't I treat you like my own child? I order you to tell me, as I should order Jeannie.'

'Well, it is – it is that you kiss Jeannie very often, and have never kissed me since the day we were just speaking of. Yet I am careful to keep my face and hands very clean, because I know that you do not like dirty children, and are always running after Jeannie to wash and comb him. But this does not make you kiss me any more, and my mother Zabelle did not kiss me either. I see that other mothers caress their children, and so I know that I am always a waif, and that you cannot forget it.'

'Come and kiss me, François,' said the miller's wife, making the child sit on her knees and kissing him with much feeling. 'It is true that I did wrong never to think of it, and you deserved better of me. You see now that I kiss you with all my heart, and you are very sure that you are not a waif, are not you?'

The child flung his arms round Madeleine's neck, and turned so pale that she was surprised, and putting him down gently from her lap, tried to distract his attention. After a minute, he left her, and ran off to hide. The miller's wife felt some uneasiness, and making a search for him, she finally found him on his knees, in a corner of the barn, bathed in tears.

'What does this mean, François?' said she, raising him up. 'I don't know what is the matter with you. If you are thinking of your poor mother Zabelle, you had better say a prayer for her, and then you will feel more at rest.'

'No, no,' said the child, twisting the end of Madeleine's apron, and kissing it with all his might. 'Are not you my mother?'

'Why are you crying then? You give me pain!'

'Oh, no! Oh, no! I am not crying,' answered François, drying his eyes quickly, and looking up cheerfully; 'I mean, I do not know why I was crying. Truly, I cannot understand it, for I am as happy as if I were in heaven.'

CHAPTER V

FROM THAT DAY ON Madeleine kissed the child, morning and evening, neither more nor less than if he had been her own, and the only difference she made between Jeannie and François was that the younger was the more petted and spoiled as became his age. He was only seven, while the waif was twelve, and François understood perfectly that a big boy like him could not be caressed like a little one. Besides, they were still more unlike in looks than in years. François was so tall and strong that he passed for fifteen, and Jeannie was small and slender like his mother, whom he greatly resembled.

It happened one morning, when she had just received François's greeting on her doorstep, and had kissed him as usual, her servant said to her:

'I mean no offence, my good mistress, but it seems to me that boy is very big to let you kiss him as if he were a little girl.'

'Do you think so?' answered Madeleine, in astonishment. 'Don't you know how young he is?'

'Yes, and I should not see any harm in it, except that he is a waif, and though I am only your servant, I would not be hired to kiss any such riff-raff.'

'What you say is wrong, Catherine,' returned Madame Blanchet; 'and above all, you should not say it before the poor child.'

'She may say it, and everybody else may say it, too,' replied François, boldly. 'I don't care; if I am not a waif for you, Madame Blanchet, I am very well satisfied.'

'Only hear him!' said the servant. 'This is the first time I ever knew him to talk so much at once. Then you know how to put two or three words together, do you, François? I really thought you could not even understand what other people said. If I had known that you were listening, I should not have spoken before you as I did, for I have no idea of hurting your feelings. You are a good, quiet, obliging boy. Come, you must not think of it any more; if it seems odd to me for our mistress to kiss you, it is only because you are too big for it, and so much coddling makes you look sillier than you really are.'

Having tried to mend matters in this way, big Catherine set about making her soup, and forgot all about what had passed.

The waif followed Madeleine to the place where she did her washing, and sitting down beside her, he spoke as he knew how to speak with her and for her alone.

'Do you remember, Madame Blanchet,' said he, 'how I was here once, long ago, and you let me go to sleep in your shawl?'

'Yes, my child,' said she, 'it was the first time we ever saw each other.'

'Was it the first time? I was not certain, for I cannot recollect very well; when I think of that time, it is all like a dream. How many years ago is it?'

'It is – wait a minute – it is nearly six years, for my Jeannie was fourteen months old.'

'So I was not so old then as he is now? When he has made his first communion, do you think he will remember all that is happening to him now?'

'Oh! Yes, I shall be sure to remember,' cried Jeannie.

'That may be so or not,' said François. 'What were you doing yesterday at this hour?'

Jeannie was startled, and opened his mouth to answer; then he stopped short, much abashed.

'Well! I wager that you cannot give a better account of yourself, either,' said the miller's wife to François. She always took pleasure in listening to the prattle of the two children.

'I?' said the waif, embarrassed. 'Wait a moment – I was going to the fields, and passed by this very place – I was thinking of you. Indeed, it was yesterday that the day when you wrapped me up in your shawl came into my mind.'

'You have a good memory, and it is surprising that you can remember so far back. Can you remember that you were ill with fever?'

'No, indeed!'

'And that you carried home my linen without my asking you?'

'No.'

'I have always remembered it, because that was the way I found out how good your heart was.'

'I have a good heart too, haven't I, mother?' said little Jeannie, presenting his mother with an apple which he had half eaten.

'To be sure you have, and you must try to copy François in all the good things you see him do.'

'Oh, yes!' answered the child quickly. 'I shall jump on the yellow colt this evening, and shall ride it into pasture.'

'Shall you?' said François, laughing. 'Are you, too, going to climb up the great ash tree to hunt tomtits? I shall let you do it, my little fellow! But listen, Madame Blanchet, there is something I want to ask of you, but I do not know whether you will tell it to me.'

'Let me hear.'

'Why do they think they hurt my feelings when they call me a waif? Is there any harm in being a waif?'

'No; certainly not, my child, since it is no fault of yours.'

'Whose fault is it?'

'It is the fault of the rich people.'

'The fault of the rich people! What does that mean?'

'You are asking a great many questions today; I shall answer you by and by.'

'No, no; right away, Madame Blanchet.'

'I cannot explain it to you. In the first place, do you know yourself what it is to be a waif?'

'Yes; it is being put in a foundling asylum by your father and mother, because they have no money to feed you and bring you up.'

'Yes, that is it. So you see that there are people so wretched as not to be able to bring up their own children, and that is the fault of the rich who do not help them.'

'You are right!' answered the waif very thoughtfully. 'Yet there are some good rich people, since you are one, Madame Blanchet, and it is only necessary to fall in their way.'

CHAPTER VI

NEVERTHELESS, THE WAIF, who was always musing and trying to find reasons for everything since he had learned to read and had made his first communion, kept pondering over what Catherine had said to Madame Blanchet about him; but it was in vain that he reflected, for he could never understand why, now that he was growing older, he should no longer kiss Madeleine. He was the most innocent boy in the world, and had no suspicion of what boys of his age learn all too quickly in the country.

His great simplicity of mind was the result of his singular bringing-up. He had never felt his position as a foundling to be a disgrace, but it had made him very shy; for though he had not taken the title as an insult, he was always surprised to find he possessed a characteristic which made a difference between himself and those with whom he associated. Foundlings are apt to be humbled by their fate, which is generally thrust upon them so harshly that they lose early their self-respect as Christians. They grow up full of hatred towards those who brought them into the world, not to speak of those who helped them to remain in it. It happened, however, that François had fallen into the hands of Zabelle, who loved him and treated him with kindness, and afterwards he had met with Madeleine, who was the most charitable and compassionate of women. She had been a good mother to him, and a waif who receives affection is better than other children, just as he is worse when he is abused and degraded.

François had never known any amusement or perfect content except when in the company of Madeleine, and instead of running off with the other shepherd-boys for his recreation, he had grown up quite solitary, or tied to the apron-strings of the two women who loved him. Especially when with Madeleine, he was as happy as Jeannie could be, and he was in no haste to play with the other children, who were sure to call him a waif, and with whom he soon felt himself a stranger, though he could not tell why.

So he reached the age of fifteen without any knowledge of wrong or conception of evil; his lips had never uttered an unclean word, nor had his ears taken in the meaning of one. Yet, since the day that Catherine had censured his mistress for the affection she showed him, the child had the great good sense and judgement to forgo his morning kiss from the miller's wife. He pretended to forget about it, or perhaps to be ashamed of being coddled like a little girl, as Catherine had said. But at the bottom, he had no such false shame, and he would have laughed at the idea, had he not guessed that the sweet woman he loved might incur blame on his account. Why should she be blamed? He could not understand it, and though he saw that he could never find it out by himself, he shrank from asking Madeleine for an explanation. He knew that her strength of love and kindness of heart had enabled her to endure the carping of others; for he had a good memory, and recollected that Madeleine had

59

been upbraided, and had narrowly escaped blows in former years because of her goodness to him.

Now, owing to his good instincts, he spared her the annoyance of being rebuked and ridiculed on his account. He understood, and it is wonderful that the poor child could understand, that a waif was to be loved only in secret; and rather than cause any trouble to Madeleine, he would have consented to do without her love.

He was attentive to his work, and as, in proportion as he grew older, he had more to do, it happened that he was less and less with Madeleine. He did not grieve for this, for, as he toiled, he said to himself that it was for her, and that he would have his reward in seeing her at meals. In the evening, when Jeannie was asleep and Catherine had gone to bed, François still stayed up with Madeleine while she worked, and read aloud to her, or talked with her. Peasants do not read very fast, so the two books they had were quite sufficient for them. When they read three pages in an evening they thought it was a great deal, and when the book was finished, so much time had passed since the beginning that they could take it up again at the first page without finding it too familiar. There are two ways of reading, and it may not be amiss to say so to those persons who think themselves well educated. Those who have much time to themselves, and many books, devour so many of them and cram so much stuff into their heads that they are utterly confused; but those who have neither leisure nor libraries are happy when a good book falls into their hands. They begin it over again a thousand times without weariness, and every time something strikes them which they had not observed before. In the main, the idea is always the same, but it is so much dwelt upon, so thoroughly enjoyed and digested, that the single mind which possesses it is better fed and more healthy than thirty thousand brains full of wind and twaddle. What I am telling you, my children, I have from the parish priest, who knows all about it.

So these two persons lived happy with what they had to consume in the matter of learning; and they consumed it slowly, helping each other to understand and love all that makes us just and good. Thus they grew in piety and courage; and they had no greater joy than to feel themselves at peace with all the world, and to be of one mind at all times and in all places, on the subject of the truth and the desire of holy living.

CHAPTER VII

MASTER BLANCHET was no longer particular concerning his household expenses, because he had fixed the amount of money which he gave to his wife every month for her housekeeping, and made it as little as possible. Madeleine could, without displeasing him, deprive herself of her own comfort in order to give alms to the poor about her; sometimes a little wood, another time part of her own dinner, again some vegetables, some clothing, some eggs, and so on. She spent all she had in the service of her neighbours, and when her money was exhausted, she did with her own hands the work of the poor, so as to save the lives of those among them who were ill and worn out. She was so economical, and mended her old clothes so carefully, that she appeared to live comfortably; and yet she was so anxious that her family should not suffer for what she gave away, that she accustomed herself to eat scarcely anything, never to rest and to sleep as little as possible. The waif saw all this, and thought it quite natural; for it was in his character, as well as in the education he received from Madeleine, to feel the same inclination, and to be drawn towards the same duty. Sometimes, only, he was troubled by the great hardships which the miller's wife endured, and blamed himself for sleeping and eating too much. He would gladly have spent the night sewing and spinning in her place; and when she tried to pay him his wages, which had risen to nearly twenty crowns, he refused to take them, and obliged her to keep them without the miller's knowledge.

'If my mother Zabelle were alive,' said he, 'this money would be for her. What do you expect me to do with it? I have no need of it, since you take care of my clothes, and provide me with sabots. Keep it for somebody more unfortunate than I am. You work so hard for the poor already, and if you give money to me, you must work still harder. If you should fall ill and die like poor Zabelle, I should like to know what good it would do me to have my chest full of money. Would it bring you back again, or prevent me from throwing myself in the river?'

'You do not know what you are talking about, my child,' said Madeleine, one day that this idea returned to his mind, as happened from time to time. 'It is not a Christian act to kill oneself, and if I should die, it would be your duty to live after me to comfort and help my Jeannie. Should not you do that for me?'

'Yes, as long as Jeannie was a child and needed my love. But afterwards! Do not let us speak of this, Madame Blanchet. I cannot be a good Christian on this point. Do not tire yourself out, and do not die, if you want me to live on this earth.'

'You may set your mind at ease, for I have no wish to die. I am well. I am hardened to work, and now I am even stronger than I was in my youth.'

'In your youth!' exclaimed François in astonishment. 'Are not you young, then?'

And he was afraid lest she might have reached the age for dying.

'I think I never had time to be young,' answered Madeleine, laughing like one who meets misfortune bravely. 'Now I am twenty-five years old, and that is a good deal for a woman of my make; for I was not born strong like you, my boy, and I have had sorrows which have aged me more than years.'

'Sorrows! Heavens, yes! I knew it very well, when Monsieur Blanchet used to speak so roughly to you. God forgive me! I am not a wicked boy, yet once when he raised his hand against you as if to strike you – Oh! He did well to change his mind, for I had seized a flail – nobody had noticed me – and I was going to fall upon him. But that was a long time ago, Madame Blanchet, for I remember that I was much shorter than he then, and now I can look right over his head. And now that he scarcely speaks to you any more, Madame Blanchet, you are no longer unhappy, are you?'

'So you think I am no longer unhappy, do you?' said Madeleine, rather sharply, thinking how it was that there had never been any love in her marriage. Then she checked herself, for what she was going to say was no concern of the waif's, and she had no right to put such ideas into a child's head.

'You are right,' said she. 'I am no longer unhappy. I live as I please. My husband is much kinder to me; my son is well and strong, and I have nothing to complain of.'

'Then don't I enter into your calculations? I—'

'You? You are well and strong, too, and that pleases me.'

'Don't I please you in any other way?'

'Yes, you are a good boy; you are always right-minded, and I am satisfied with you.'

'Oh! If you were not satisfied with me, what a scamp, what a good-for-nothing I should be, after the way in which you have treated me! But there is still something else which ought to make you happy, if you think as I do.'

'Very well, tell me; for I do not know what puzzle you are contriving for me.'

'I mean no puzzle, Madame Blanche! I need but look into my heart, and I see that even if I had to suffer hunger, thirst, heat and cold, and were to be beaten half to death every day into the bargain, and then had only a bundle of thorns or a heap of stones to lie on – well, can you understand?'

'I think so, my dear François; you could be happy in spite of so much evil if only your heart were at peace with God.'

'Of course that is true, and I need not speak of it. But I meant something else.'

'I cannot imagine what you are aiming at, and I see that you are cleverer than I am.'

'No, I am not clever. I mean that I could suffer all the pains that a man living mortal life can endure, and could still be happy if I thought Madame Blanchet loved me. That is the reason why I just said to you that if you thought as I did, you would say: "François loves me, and I am content to be alive."'

'You are right, my poor dear child,' answered Madeleine; 'and the things you say to me sometimes make me want to cry. Yes, truly, your affection for me is one of the joys of my life, and perhaps the greatest, after – no, I mean with my Jeannie's. As you are older than he, you can understand better what I say to you, and you can better explain your thoughts to me. I assure you that I am never wearied when I am with both of you, and the only prayer I make to God is that we may long be able to live together as we do now, without separating.'

'Without separating, I should think so!' said François. 'I should rather be cut into little pieces than leave you. Who else would love me as you have loved me? Who would run the danger of being ill-treated for the sake of a poor waif, and who would call me her child, her dear son? For you call me so often, almost always. You often say to me when we are alone: "Call me *mother*, and not always Madame Blanchet." I do not dare to do so, because I am afraid of becoming accustomed to it and letting it slip out before somebody.'

'Well, even if you did so?'

'Oh! You would be sure to be blamed for it, and I do not like to have you tormented on my account. I am not proud, and I do not care to have it known that you have raised me from my orphan estate. I am satisfied to know, all by myself, that I have a mother and am her child. Oh! You must not die, Madame Blanchet,' added poor François, looking at her sadly, for his thoughts had long been running on possible calamity. 'If I lost you, I should have no other friend on this earth; you would go straight into Paradise, and I am not sure that I deserve ever to receive the reward of going there with you.'

François had a kind of foreboding of heavy misfortune in all he said and thought, and some little time afterwards the misfortune fell.

He had become the servant of the mill, and it was his duty to make the round of the customers of the mill, to carry their corn away on his horse, and return it to them in flour. This sometimes obliged him to take long rides, and for this same purpose he often visited Blanchet's mistress, who lived about a league from the mill. He was not at all fond of this commission, and would never linger an instant in her house after her corn was weighed and measured.

* * * * * * * *

At this point of the tale the narrator stopped.

'Are you aware that I have been talking a long time?' said she to her friends, who were listening. 'My lungs are not so strong as they once were, and I think that the hemp-dresser, who knows the story better than I, might relieve me, especially as we have just come to a place that I do not remember so well.'

'I know why your memory is not so good in the middle as in the beginning,' answered the hemp-dresser. 'It is because the waif is about to get into trouble, and you cannot stand it, because you are chicken-hearted about love stories, like all other pious women.'

'Is this going to turn into a love story?' asked Sylvine Courtioux, who happened to be present.

'Good!' replied the hemp-dresser. 'I knew that if I let out that word all the young girls would prick up their ears. But you must have patience; the part of the story which I am going to take up on condition that I may carry it to a happy close is not yet what you want to hear. Where had you come to, Mother Monique?'

'I had come to Blanchet's mistress.'

'That was it,' said the hemp-dresser. The woman was called Sévère, but her name was not well suited to her, for there was nothing to match it in her disposition. She was very clever about hoodwinking people when she wanted to get money out of them. She cannot be called entirely bad, for she was of a joyous, careless temper; but she thought only of herself, and cared not at all for the loss of others, provided that she had all the finery and recreation she wanted. She had been the fashion in the country, and it was said that she had found many men to her taste. She was still a very handsome, buxom woman, alert though stout, and rosy as a cherry. She paid but little attention to the waif, and if she met him in her barn or courtyard she made fun of him with some nonsense or other, but without malicious intent and for the pleasure of seeing him blush; for he blushed like a girl, and was ill at ease whenever she spoke to him. He thought her brazen, and she seemed both ugly and wicked in his eyes, though she was neither one nor the other; at least, she was only spiteful when she was crossed in her interests or her vanity, and I must even acknowledge that she liked to give almost as much as to receive. She was ostentatiously generous, and enjoyed being thanked; but to the mind of the waif she was a devil, who reduced Madame Blanchet to want and drudgery.

Nevertheless, it happened that when the waif was seventeen years old, Madame Sévère discovered that he was a deucedly handsome fellow. He was not like most country boys, who, at his age, are dumpy and thickset, and only develop into something worth looking at two or three years later. He was already tall and well-built; his skin was white, even at harvest time, and his tight curling hair was brown at the roots and golden at the ends.

'Do you admire that sort of thing, Madame Monique? I mean the hair, without any reference to boys.'

'That is no business of yours,' answered the priest's servant. 'Go on with your story.'

He was always poorly dressed, but he loved cleanliness, as Madeleine Blanchet had taught him; and such as he was, he had an air that no one else had. Sévère noticed this little by little, and finally she was so well aware of it that she took it into her head to thaw him out a little. She was not a woman of prejudice, and when she heard anybody say, 'What a pity that such a handsome boy should be a waif!' she answered. 'There is every reason that waifs should be handsome, for love brought them into the world.'

She devised the following plan for being in his company. She made Blanchet drink immoderately at the fair of Saint-Denis-de-Jouhet, and when she saw that he was no longer able to put one foot before the other, she asked the friends she had in the place to put him to bed. Then she said to François, who had come with his master to drive his animals to the fair:

'My lad, I am going to leave my mare for your master to return with tomorrow morning; you may mount his and take me home on the crupper.'

This arrangement was not at all to François's taste. He said that the mare that belonged to the mill was not strong enough to carry two people, and he offered to accompany Sévère home, if she rode her own horse and allowed him to ride Blanchet's. He promised to come back immediately with a fresh mount for his master, and to reach Saint-Denis-de-Jouhet early the next morning; but Sévère would listen to him no more than the wind, and ordered him to obey her. François was afraid of her; for, as Blanchet saw with no eyes but hers, she could have him sent away from the mill if he displeased her, especially as the feast of St John was near at hand. So he took her up behind him, without suspecting, poor fellow, that this was not the best means of escaping his evil destiny.

CHAPTER VIII

I T WAS TWILIGHT when they set out, and when they passed the sluice of the pond of Rochefolle night had already fallen. The moon had not yet risen above the trees, and in that part of the country the roads are so washed by numerous springs that they are not at all good. François spurred his mare on to speed, for he disliked the company of Sévère, and longed to be with Madame Blanchet.

But Sévère, who was in no haste to reach home, began to play the part of a fine lady, saying that she was afraid, and that the mare must not go faster than a walk, because she did not lift her legs well and might stumble at any minute.

'Bah!' said François, without paying any attention. 'Then it would be the first time she said her prayers, for I never saw a mare so disinclined to piety!'

'You are witty, François,' said Sévère, giggling, as if François had said something very new and amusing.

'Oh, no indeed!' answered the waif, who thought she was laughing at him.

'Come,' said she, 'you surely cannot mean to trot downhill?'

'You need not fear, for we can trot perfectly well.'

The trot downhill stopped the stout Sévère's breath, and prevented her talking. She was extremely vexed, as she had expected to coax the young man with her soft words, but she was unwilling to let him see that she was neither young nor slender enough to stand fatigue, and was silent for a part of the way.

When they came to a chestnut grove, she took it into her head to say: 'Stop, François; you must stop, dear François. The mare has just lost a shoe.'

'Even if she has lost a shoe,' said François, 'I have neither hammer nor nails to put it on with.'

'But we must not lose the shoe. It is worth something! Get down, I say, and look for it.'

'I might look two hours for it, among these ferns, without finding it. And my eyes are not lanterns.'

'Oh, yes, François,' said Sévère, half in jest and half in earnest; 'your eyes shine like glow-worms.'

'Then you can see them through my hat, I suppose?' answered François, not at all pleased with what he took for derision.

'I cannot see them just now,' said Sévère with a sigh as big as herself, 'but I have seen them at other times!'

'You can never have seen anything amiss in them,' returned the innocent waif. 'You may as well leave them alone, for they have never looked rudely at you and never will.'

'I think,' broke in at this moment the priest's servant, 'that you might skip this part of the story. It is not very interesting to hear all the bad devices of this wicked woman, for ensnaring our waif.'

'Put yourself at ease, Mother Monique,' replied the hemp-dresser. 'I shall skip as much as is proper. I know that I am speaking before young people, and I shall not say a word too much.'

We were just speaking of François's eyes, the expression of which Sévère was trying to make less irreproachable than he had declared it to be.

'How old are you, François?' said she with more politeness, so as to let him understand that she was no longer going to treat him like a little boy.

'Oh, Heavens! I don't know exactly,' answered the waif, beginning to perceive her clumsy advances. 'I do not often amuse myself by reckoning my years.'

'I heard that you were only seventeen,' she resumed, 'but I wager that you must be twenty, for you are tall, and will soon have a beard on your chin.'

'It is all the same to me,' said François, yawning.

'Take care! You are going too fast, my boy. There! I have just lost my purse!'

'The deuce you have!' said François, who had not as yet discovered how shy she was. 'Then I suppose that you must get off and look for it, for it may be of value.'

He jumped down and helped her to dismount. She took pains to lean against him, and he found her heavier than a sack of corn.

While she pretended to search for the purse, which was all the time in her pocket, he went on five or six steps, holding the mare by the bridle.

'Are not you going to help me look for it?' said she.

'I must hold the mare,' said he, 'for she is thinking of her colt, and if I let her loose she will run home.'

Sévère looked under the mare's leg, close beside François, and from this he saw that she had lost nothing except her senses.

'We had not come as far as this,' said he, 'when you called out that you had lost your purse. So you certainly cannot find it here.'

'Do you think I am shamming, you rogue?' said she, trying to pull his ear. 'For I really believe that you are a rogue.'

François drew back, as he was in no mood for a frolic.

'No, no,' said he, 'if you have found your money, let us go, for I should rather be asleep than stay here jesting.'

'Then we can talk,' said Sévère, when she was seated again behind him. 'They say that beguiles the weariness of the road.'

'I need no beguiling,' answered the waif, 'for I am not weary.'

'That is the first pretty speech you have made me, François!'

'If it is a pretty speech, I made it by accident, for I do not understand that sort of thing.'

Sévère was exasperated, but she would not as yet give in to the truth.

'The boy must be a simpleton,' said she to herself. 'If I make him lose his way, he will have to stay a little longer with me.'

So she tried to mislead him, and to induce him to turn to the left when he was going to the right.

'You are making a mistake,' said she. 'This is the first time you have been over this road. I know it better than you do. Take my advice, or you will make me spend the night in the woods, young man!'

When François had once been over a road, he knew it so perfectly that he could find his way in it at the end of a year.

'No, no,' said he, 'this is the right way, and I am not in the least out of my head. The mare knows it too, and I have no desire to spend the night rambling about the woods.'

Thus he reached the farm of Dollins, where Sévère lived, without losing a quarter of an hour and without giving an opening as wide as the eye of a needle to her advances. Once there, she tried to detain him, insisting that the night was dark, that the water had risen, and that he would have difficulty in crossing the fords. The waif cared not a whit for these dangers, and, bored with so many foolish words, he struck the mare with his heels, galloped off without waiting to hear the rest, and returned swiftly to the mill, where Madeleine Blanchet was waiting for him, grieved that he should come so late.

CHAPTER IX

THE WAIF NEVER told Madeleine what Sévère had given him to understand; he would not have dared, and indeed dared not even think of it himself. I cannot say that I should have behaved as discreetly as he in such an adventure; but a little discretion never does any harm, and then I am telling things as they happened. This boy was as refined as a well-brought-up girl.

As Madame Sévère thought over the matter at night, she became incensed against him, and perceived that he had scorned her and was not the fool she had taken him for. Chafing at this thought, her spleen rose, and great projects of revenge passed through her head.

So much so that when Cadet Blanchet, still half drunk, returned to her next morning, she gave him to understand that his mill-boy was a little upstart, whom she had been obliged to hold in check and cuff in the face, because he had taken it into his head to make love to her and kiss her as they came home together through the wood at night.

This was more than enough to disorder Blanchet's wits; but she was not yet satisfied, and jeered at him for leaving at home with his wife a fellow who would be inclined by his age and character to beguile the dullness of her life.

In the twinkling of an eye, Blanchet was jealous both of his mistress and his wife. He seized his heavy stick, pulled his hat down over his eyes, like an extinguisher on a candle, and rushed off to the mill, without stopping for breath.

Fortunately, the waif was not there. He had gone away to fell and saw up a tree that Blanchet had bought from Blanchard of Guérin, and was not to return till evening. Blanchet would have gone to find him at his work, but he shrank from showing his fury before the young millers of Guérin, lest they should make sport of him for his jealousy, which was unreasonable after his long neglect and contempt of his wife.

He would have stayed to wait for his return, but he thought it too wearisome to stay all day at home, and he knew that the quarrel which he wished to pick with his wife could not last long enough to occupy him till evening. It is impossible to be angry very long when the ill temper is all on one side.

In spite of this, however, he could have endured all the derision and the tedium for the pleasure of belabouring the poor waif; but as his walk had cooled him to some degree, he reflected that this cursed waif was no longer a child, and that if he were old enough to think of making love, he was also old enough to defend himself with blows, if provoked. So he tried to gather his wits together, drinking glass after glass in silence, revolving in his brain what he was going to say to his wife, but did not know how to begin.

He had said roughly, on entering, that he wished her to listen to something; so she sat near him, as usual sad, silent, and with a tinge of pride in her manner.

'Madame Blanchet,' said he at last, 'I have a command to give you, but if you were the woman you pretend to be, and that you have the reputation of being, you would not wait to be told.'

There he halted as if to take breath, but the fact is that he was almost ashamed of what he was going to say, for virtue was written on his wife's face as plainly as a prayer in a missal.

Madeleine would not help him to explain himself. She did not breathe a word, but waited for him to go on, expecting him to find fault with her for some expenditure, for she had no suspicion of what he was meditating.

'You behave as if you did not understand me, Madame Blanchet,' continued the miller, 'and yet my meaning is clear. You must throw that rubbish out of doors, the sooner the better, for I have had enough and too much of all this sort of thing.'

'Throw what?' asked Madeleine, in amazement.

'Throw what! Then you do not dare to say throw *whom*?'

'Good God! No; I know nothing about it,' said she. 'Speak, if you want me to understand you.'

'You will make me lose my temper,' cried Cadet Blanchet, bellowing like a bull. 'I tell you that waif is not wanted in my house, and if he is still here by tomorrow morning, I shall turn him out of doors by main force, unless he prefer to take a turn under my mill wheel.'

'Your words are cruel, and your purpose is very foolish, Master Blanchet,' said Madeleine, who could not help turning as white as her cap. 'You will ruin your business if you send the boy away; for you will never find another who will work so well, and be satisfied with such small wages. What has the poor child done to make you want to drive him away so cruelly?'

'He makes a fool of me, I tell you, Madame Wife, and I do not intend to be the laughing stock of the country. He has made himself master of my house, and deserves to be paid with a cudgel for what he has done.'

It was some time before Madeleine could understand what her husband meant. She had not the slightest conception of it, and brought forward all the reasons she could think of to appease him and prevent his persisting in his caprice.

It was all labour lost, for he only grew the more furious; and when he saw how grieved she was to lose her good servant François, he had a fresh access of jealousy, and spoke so brutally that his meaning dawned on her at last, and she began to cry from mortification, injured pride and bitter sorrow.

This did not mend matters; Blanchet swore that she was in love with this bundle of goods from the asylum, that he blushed for her, and that if she did not turn the waif out of doors without delay, he would kill him and grind him to powder.

Thereupon she answered more haughtily than was her wont that he had the right to send away whom he chose from his house, but not to wound and insult his faithful wife, and that she would complain to God and all the saints of Heaven of his cruel and intolerable injustice. Thus, in spite of herself, she came gradually to reproach him with his evil behaviour, and confronted him with the plain feet that if a man is dissatisfied with his own cap, he tries to throw his neighbour's into the mud.

It went from bad to worse, and when Blanchet finally perceived that he was in the wrong, anger was his only resource. He threatened to shut Madeleine's mouth with a blow, and would have done so if Jeannie had not heard the noise and come running in between them, without understanding what the matter was, but quite pale and discomfited by so much wrangling. When Blanchet ordered him away, the child cried, and his father took occasion to say that he was ill-brought-up, a cry-baby and a coward, and that his mother would never be able to make anything out of him. Then Blanchet plucked up courage, and rose, brandishing his stick, and swearing that he would kill the waif.

When Madeleine saw that he was mad with passion, she threw herself boldly in front of him, and he, disconcerted and taken by surprise, allowed her her way. She snatched his stick out of his hands and threw it far off into the river, and then, standing her ground, she said:

'You shall not ruin yourself by obeying this wicked impulse. Reflect that calamity is swift to follow a man who loses his self-control, and if you have no feeling for others, think of yourself and the probable consequences of a single bad action. For a long time you have been guiding your life amiss, my husband, and now you are hastening faster and faster along a dangerous road. I shall prevent you, at least for today, from committing a worse crime, which would bring its punishment both in this world and the next. You shall not kill; return to where you came from, rather than persevere in trying to revenge yourself for an affront which was not offered. Go away; I command you to do so in your own interest, and this is the first time in my life that I have ever commanded you to do anything. You will obey me, because you will see that I still observe the deference I owe you. I swear to you on my word and honour that the waif shall not be here tomorrow, and that you may come back without any fear of meeting him.'

Having said this, Madeleine opened the door of the house for her husband, and Cadet Blanchet, baffled by the novelty of her manner, and pleased in the main to receive her submission without danger to his person, clapped his hat upon his head, and, without another word, returned to Sévère. He did not fail to boast to her and to others that he had administered a sound thrashing to his wife and to the waif; but as this was not true, Sévère's pleasure evaporated in smoke.

When Madeleine Blanchet was alone again, she sent Jeannie to drive the sheep and the goat to pasture, and went off to a little lonely nook beside the mill-dam, where the earth was much eaten away by the force of the current, and the place so crowded with a fresh growth of branches above the old tree-stumps that you could not see two steps away from you. She was in the habit of going there to pray, for nobody could interrupt her, and she could be as entirely concealed behind the tall weeds as a water hen in its nest of green leaves.

As soon as she reached there, she sank on her knees to seek in prayer the relief she so needed. But though she hoped this would bring great comfort, she could think of nothing but the poor waif, who was to be sent sway, and who loved her so that he would die of grief. So nothing came to her lips, except that she was most unhappy to lose her only support and separate herself from the child of her heart. Then she cried so long and so bitterly that she was suffocated, and, falling full length along the grass, lay unconscious for more than an hour, and it is a miracle that she ever came to herself.

At nightfall she made an effort to collect her powers; and when she heard Jeannie come home singing with the flock, she rose with difficulty and set about preparing supper. Shortly afterwards, she heard the noise of the return of the oxen, who were drawing home the oak tree that Blanchet had bought, and Jeannie ran joyfully to meet his friend François, whose presence he had missed all day. Poor little Jeannie had been grieved for a moment by his father's cruel behaviour to his dear mother, and he had run off to cry in the fields, without knowing what the quarrel could be. But a child's sorrow lasts no longer than the dew of the morning, and he had already forgotten his trouble. He took François by the hand, and skipping as gaily as a little partridge, brought him to Madeleine.

There was no need for the waif to look twice to see that her eyes were reddened and her face blanched.

'Good God,' thought he, 'some misfortune has happened.' Then he turned pale too, and trembled, fixing his eyes on Madeleine, and expecting her to speak to him. She made him sit down, and set his meal before him in silence, but he could not swallow a mouthful. Jeannie ate and prattled on by himself; he felt no uneasiness, for his mother kissed him from time to time and encouraged him to make a good supper.

When he had gone to bed, and the servant was putting the room in order, Madeleine went out, and beckoned François to follow her. She walked through the meadow as far as the fountain, and then calling all her courage to her aid, she said:

'My child, misfortune has fallen upon you and me, and God strikes us both a heavy blow. You see how much I suffer, and out of love for me, try to strengthen your own heart, for if you do not uphold me, I cannot tell what will become of me.'

François guessed nothing, although he at once supposed that the trouble came from Monsieur Blanchet.

'What are you saying?' said he to Madeleine, kissing her hands as if she were his mother. 'How can you think that I shall not have courage to comfort and sustain you? Am not I your servant for as long as I have to stay upon the earth? Am not I your child, who will work for you, and is now strong enough to keep you from want? Leave Monsieur Blanchet alone, let him squander his money, since it is his choice. I shall feed and clothe both you and our Jeannie. If I must leave you for a time, I shall go and hire myself out, though not far from here, so that I can see you every day, and come and spend Sundays with you. I am strong enough now to work and earn all the money you need. You are so careful and live on so little. Now you will not be able to deny yourself so many things for others, and you will be the better for it. Come, Madame Blanchet, my dear mother, calm yourself and do not cry, or I think I shall die of grief.'

When Madeleine saw that he had not understood, and that she must tell him everything, she commended her soul to God, and made up her mind to inflict this great pain upon him.

CHAPTER X

'NO, FRANÇOIS, my son,' said she, 'that is not it. My husband is not yet ruined, as far as I know anything of his affairs, and if it were only the fear of want, you would not see me so unhappy. Nobody need dread poverty who has courage to work. Since you must hear why it is that I am so sick at heart, let me tell you that Monsieur Blanchet is in a fury against you, and will no longer endure your presence in his house.'

'Is that it?' cried François, springing up. 'He may as well kill me outright, as I cannot live after such a blow. Yes, let him put an end to me, for he has long disliked me and longed to have me die, I know. Let me see, where is he? I will go to him and say, "Tell me why you drive me away, and perhaps I can prove to you that you are mistaken in your reasons. But if you persist, say so, that – that…" I do not know what I am saying, Madeleine; truly, I do not know; I have lost my senses, and I can no longer see clearly; my heart is pierced and my head is turning I am sure I shall either die or go mad.'

The poor waif threw himself on the ground, and struck his head with his fists, as he had done when Zabelle had tried to take him back to the asylum.

When Madeleine saw this, her high spirit returned. She took him by the hands and arms, and shaking him, forced him to listen to her.

'If you have no more resignation and strength of will than a child,' said she, 'you do not deserve my love, and you will shame me for bringing you up as my son. Get up. You are a man in years, and a man should not roll on the ground, as you are doing. Listen, François, and tell me whether you love me enough to go without seeing me for a time. Look, my child, it is for my peace and good name, for otherwise my husband will subject me to annoyance and humiliation. So you must leave me today, out of love, just as I have kept you, out of love, to this day; for love shows itself in different ways according to time and circumstance. You must leave me without delay, because, in order to prevent Monsieur Blanchet from committing a crime, I promised that you should be gone tomorrow morning. Tomorrow is St John's day, and you must go and find a place; but not too near at hand, for if we were able to see each other every day, it would be all the worse in Monsieur Blanchet's mind.'

'What has he in his mind, Madeleine? Of what does he complain? How have I behaved amiss? Does he think that you rob the house to help me? That cannot be, because now I am one of his household. I eat only enough to satisfy my hunger, and I do not steal a pin from him. Perhaps he thinks that I take my wages, and that I cost him too much. Very well, let me follow out my purpose of going to explain to him that since my poor mother Zabelle died, I have never received a single penny; or, if you do not want me to tell him this – and indeed if he knew it, he would try to make you pay back all the money due on my wages that you have spent in charity – well, I will make him this proposition for the next year. I will offer to remain in your service for nothing. In this way he cannot think me a burden, and will allow me to stay with you.'

'No, no, no, François,' cried Madeleine, hastily, 'it is not possible; and if you said this to him, he would fly into such a rage with you and me that worse would come of it.'

'But why?' asked François. 'What is he angry about? Is it only for the pleasure of making us unhappy that he pretends to mistrust me?'

'My child, do not ask the reason of his anger, for I cannot tell you. I should be too much ashamed, and you had better not even try to guess; but I can assure you that your duty towards me is to go away. You are tall and strong, and can do without me; and you will earn your living better elsewhere, as long as you will take nothing from me. All sons have to leave their mothers when they go out to work, and many go far away. You must go like the rest, and I shall grieve as all mothers do. I shall weep for you and think of you, and pray God morning and evening to shield you from all ill.'

'Yes, and you will take another servant who will serve you ill, who will take no care of your son or your property, who will perhaps hate you, if Monsieur Blanchet orders him not to obey you, and will repeat and misrepresent to him all the kind things you do. You may be unhappy, and I shall not be with you to protect and comfort you. Ah! You think that I have no courage because I am miserable? You believe that I am thinking only of myself, and tell me that I shall earn more money elsewhere! I am not thinking of myself at all. What is it to me whether I gain or lose? I do not even care to know whether I shall be able to control my despair. I shall live or die as may please God, and it makes no difference to me, as long as I am prevented from devoting my life to you. What gives me intolerable anguish is that I see trouble ahead for you. You will be trampled upon in your turn, and if Monsieur Blanchet puts me out of the way, it is that he may the more easily walk over your rights.'

'Even if God permits this,' said Madeleine, 'I must bear what I cannot help. It is wrong to make one's fate worse by kicking against the pricks. You know that I am very unhappy, and you may imagine how much more wretched I should be if I learned that you were ill, disgusted with life and unwilling to be comforted. But if I can find any consolation in my affliction, it will be because I hear that you are well behaved, and keep up your health and courage out of love for me.'

This last excellent reason gave Madeleine the advantage. The waif gave in, and promised on his knees, as if in the confessional, that he would do his best to bear his sorrow bravely.

'Then,' said he, as he wiped his eyes, 'if I must go tomorrow morning, I shall say good-by to you now, my mother Madeleine. Farewell, for this life, perhaps; for you do not tell me if I shall ever see you and talk with you again. If you do not think I shall ever have such happiness, do not say so, for I should lose courage to live. Let me keep the hope of meeting you one day here by this clear fountain, where I met you the first time nearly eleven years ago. From that day to this, I have had nothing but happiness; I must not forget all the joys that God has given me through you, but shall keep them in remembrance, so that they may help me to bear, from tomorrow onwards, all that time and fate may bring. I carry away a heart pierced and benumbed with anguish, knowing that you are unhappy, and that in me you lose your best friend. You tell me that your distress will be greater if I do not take heart, so I shall sustain myself as best I may, by thoughts of you, and I value your affection too much to forfeit it by cowardice. Farewell, Madame Blanchet; leave me here alone a little while; I shall feel better when I have cried my fill. If any of my tears fall into this fountain, you will think of me whenever you come to wash here. I am going to gather some of this mint to perfume my linen. I must soon pack my bundle; and as long as I smell the sweet fragrance among my clothes, I shall imagine that I am here and see you before me. Farewell, farewell, my dear mother; I shall not go back with you to the house. I might kiss little Jeannie, without waking him, but I have not the heart. You must kiss him for me; and to keep him from crying, please tell him tomorrow that I am coming back soon. So, while he is expecting me, he will have time to forget me a little; and then later, you must talk to him of poor François, so that he may not forget me too much. Give me your blessing, Madeleine, as you gave it to me on the day of my first communion, for it will bring with it the grace of God.'

The poor waif knelt down before Madeleine, entreating her to forgive him if he had ever offended her against his will.

Madeleine declared that she had nothing to forgive him, and that she wished her blessing could prove as beneficent as that of God.

'Now,' said François, 'that I am again a waif, and that nobody will ever love me any more, will not you kiss me as you once kissed me, in kindness, on the day of my first communion? I shall need to remember this, so that I may be very sure that you still love me in your heart, like a mother.'

Madeleine kissed the waif in the same pure spirit as when he was a little child. Yet anybody who had seen her would have fancied there was some justification for Monsieur Blanchet's anger, and would have blamed this faithful woman, who had no thought of ill, and whose action could not have displeased the Virgin Mary.

'Nor me, either,' put in the priest's servant.

'And me still less,' returned the hemp-dresser. Then he resumed:

She returned to the house, but not to sleep. She heard François come in and do up his bundle in the next room, and she heard him go out again at daybreak. She did not get up till he had gone some little distance, so as not to weaken his courage, but when she heard his steps on the little bridge, she opened the door a crack, without allowing herself to be seen, so that she might catch one more last glimpse of him. She saw him stop and look back at the river and mill, as if to bid them farewell. Then he strode away very rapidly, after first picking a branch of poplar and putting it in his hat, as men do when they go out for hire, to show that they are trying to find a place.

Master Blanchet came in towards noon, but did not speak till his wife said:

'You must go out and hire another boy for your mill, for François has gone, and you are without a servant.'

'That is quite enough, wife,' answered Blanchet. 'I shall go, but I warn you not to expect another young fellow.'

As these were all the thanks he gave her for her submission, her feelings were so much wounded that she could not help showing it.

'Cadet Blanchet,' said she, 'I have obeyed your will; I have sent an excellent boy away without a motive, and I must confess that I did so with regret. I do not ask for your gratitude, but, in my turn, I have something to command you, and that is not to insult me, for I do not deserve it.'

She said this in a manner so new to Blanchet, that it produced its effect on him.

'Come, wife,' said he, holding out his hand to her, 'let us make a truce to all this, and think no more about it. Perhaps I may have been a little hasty in what I said; but you see I had my own reasons for not trusting the waif. The devil is the father of all those children, and he is always after them. They may be good in some ways, but they are sure to be scamps in others. I know that it will be hard for me to find another such hard worker for a servant; but the devil, who is a good father, had whispered wantonness into that boy's ear, and I know one woman who had a complaint against him.'

'That woman is not your wife,' rejoined Madeleine, 'and she may be lying. Even if she told the truth, that would be no cause for suspecting me.'

'Do I suspect you?' said Blanchet, shrugging his shoulders. 'My grudge was only against him, and now that he has gone, I have forgotten about it. If I said anything displeasing to you, you must take it in jest.'

'Such jests are not to my taste,' answered Madeleine. 'Keep them for those who like them.'

CHAPTER XI

MADELEINE BORE HER sorrow very well at first. She heard from her new servant, who had met with François, that he had been hired for eighteen pistoles a year by a farmer, who had a good mill and some land over towards Aigurande. She was happy to know that he had found a good place, and did her utmost to return to her occupations, without grieving too much. In spite of her efforts, however, she fell ill for a long time of a low fever, and pined quietly away, without anybody's noticing it. François was right when he said that in him she lost her best friend. She was sad and lonely, and, having nobody to talk with, she petted all the more her son Jeannie, who was a very nice boy, as gentle as a lamb.

But he was too young to understand all that she had to say of François, and, besides, he showed her no such kind cares and attentions as the waif had done at his age. Jeannie loved his mother, more even than children ordinarily do, because she was such a mother as is hard to find; but he never felt the same wonder and emotion about her as François did. He thought it quite natural to be so tenderly loved and caressed. He received it as his portion, and counted on it as his due, whereas the waif had never been unmindful of the slightest kindness from her, and made his gratitude so apparent in his behaviour, his words and looks, his blushes and tears, that when Madeleine was with him she forgot that her home was bereft of peace, love and comfort.

When she was left again forlorn, all this evil returned upon her, and she meditated long on the sorrows which François's affectionate companionship had kept in abeyance. Now she had nobody to read with her, to help her in caring for the poor, to pray with her, or even now and then to exchange a few frank, good-natured jests with her. Nothing that she saw or did gave her any more pleasure, and her thoughts wandered back to the time when she had with her such a kind, gentle and loving friend. Whether she went into her vineyard, into her orchard or into the mill, there was not a spot as large as a pocket handkerchief that she had not passed over ten thousand times, with this child clinging to her skirts, or this faithful, zealous friend at her side. It was as if she had lost a son of great worth and promise; and it was in vain she heaped her affection on the one who still remained, for half her heart was left untenanted.

Her husband saw that she was wearing away, and felt some pity for her languid, melancholy looks. He feared lest she might fall seriously ill, and was loath to lose her, as she was a skilful manager, and saved on her side as much as he wasted on his. As Sévère would not allow him to attend to his mill, he knew that his business would go to pieces if Madeleine no longer had the charge of it, and though he continued to upbraid her from habit, and complained of her lack of care, he knew that nobody else would serve him better.

He exerted himself to contrive some means of curing her of her sickness and sorrow, and just at this juncture it happened that his uncle died. His youngest sister had been under this uncle's guardianship, and now she fell into his own care. He thought, at first, of sending the girl to live with Sévère, but his other relations made him ashamed of this project; and, besides, when Sévère found that the girl was only just fifteen, and promised to be as fair as the day, she had no further desire to be entrusted with such a charge, and told Blanchet that she was afraid of the risks attendant on the care of a young girl.

So Blanchet – who saw that he should gain something by being his sister's guardian, as the uncle, who had brought her up, had left her money in his will; and who was unwilling to place her with any of his other relations – brought her home to his mill, and requested his wife to treat her as a sister and companion, to teach her to work, and let her share in the household labours, and yet to make the task so easy that she should have no desire to go elsewhere.

Madeleine acquiesced gladly in this family arrangement. She liked Mariette Blanchet from the first for the sake of her beauty, the very cause for which Sévère had disliked her. She believed, too, that a sweet disposition and a good heart always go with a pretty face, and she received the young girl not so much as a sister as a daughter, who might perhaps take the place of poor François.

During all this time poor François bore his trouble with as much patience as he had, and this was none at all; for never was man nor boy visited with so heavy an affliction. He fell ill, in the first place, and this was almost fortunate for him, for it proved the kindness of his master's family, who would not allow him to be sent to the hospital, but kept him at home, and tended him carefully. The miller, his present master, was most unlike Cadet Blanchet, and his daughter, who was about thirty years old, and not yet married, had a reputation for her charities and good conduct.

These good people plainly saw, too, in spite of the waif's illness, that they had found a treasure in him.

He was so strong and well-built that he threw off his disease more quickly than most people, and though he set to work before he was cured, he had no relapse. His conscience spurred him on to make up for lost time and repay his master and mistress for their kindness. He still felt ill for more than two months, and every morning, when he began his work, he was as giddy as if he had just fallen from the roof of a house, but little by little he warmed up to it, and never told the trouble it cost him to begin. The miller and his daughter were so well pleased with him that they entrusted him with the management of many things which were far above his position. When they found that he could read and write, they made him keep the accounts, which had never been kept before, and the need of which had often involved the mill in difficulties. In short, he was as well off as was compatible with his misfortune; and as he had the prudence to refrain from saying that he was a foundling, nobody reproached him with his origin.

But neither the kind treatment he received, nor his work, nor his illness, could make him forget Madeleine, his dear mill at Cormouer, his little Jeannie and the graveyard where Zabelle was lying. His heart was always far away, and on Sundays he did nothing but brood, and so had no rest from the labours of the week. He was at such a distance from his home, which was more than six leagues off, that no news from it ever reached him. He thought at first that he would become used to this, but he was consumed with anxiety, and tried to invent means of finding out about Madeleine, at least twice a year. He went to the fairs for the purpose of meeting some acquaintance from the old place, and if he saw one, he made inquiries about all his friends, beginning prudently with those for whom he cared least, and leading up to Madeleine, who interested him most; and thus he had some tidings of her and her family.

'But it is growing late, my friends, and I am going to sleep in the middle of my story. I shall go on with it tomorrow, if you care to hear it Goodnight, all.'

The hemp-dresser went off to bed, and the farmer lit his lantern and took Mother Monique back to the parsonage, for she was an old woman, and could not see her way clearly.

CHAPTER XII

T HE NEXT EVENING we all met again at the farm, and the hemp-dresser resumed his story:

François had been living about three years in the country of Aigurande, near Villechiron, in a handsome mill which is called Haut-Champault, or Bas-Champault, or Frechampault, for Champault is as common a name in that country as in our own. I have been twice into those parts, and know what a fine country it is. The peasants there are richer, and better lodged and fed; there is more business there, and though the earth is less fertile, it is more productive. The land is more broken; it is pierced by rocks and washed by torrents, but it is fair and pleasant to the eye. The trees are marvellously beautiful, and two streams, clear as crystal, rush noisily along through their deep-cut channels.

The mills there are more considerable than ours, and the one where François lived was among the richest and best. One winter day, his master, by name Jean Vertaud, said to him:

'François, my servant and friend, I have something to say to you, and I ask for your attention.

'You and I have known each other for some little time. I have done very well in my business, and my mill has prospered; I have succeeded better than others of my trade; in short, my fortune has increased, and I do not conceal from myself that I owe it all to you. You have served me not as a servant, but as a friend and relation. You have devoted yourself to my interests as if they were your own. You have managed my property better than I knew how to do myself, and have shown yourself possessed of more knowledge and intelligence than I. I am not suspicious by nature, and I should have been often cheated if you had not kept watch of all the people and things about me. Those who were in the habit of abusing my good nature complained, and you bore the brunt boldly, though more than once you exposed yourself to dangers, which you escaped only by your courage and gentleness. What I like most about you is that your heart is as good as your head and hand. You love order, but not avarice. You do not allow yourself to be duped, as I do, and yet you are as fond of helping your neighbour as I can be. You were the first to advise me to be generous in real cases of need, but you were quick to hold me back from giving to those who were merely making a pretence of distress. You have sense and originality. The ideas you put into practice are always successful, and whatever you touch turns to good account.

'I am well pleased with you, and I should like, on my part, to do something for you. Tell me frankly what you want, for I shall refuse you nothing.'

'I do not know why you say this,' answered François. 'You must think, Master Vertaud, that I am dissatisfied with you, but it is not so. You may be sure of that.'

'I do not say that you are dissatisfied, but you do not generally look like a happy man. Your spirits are not good. You never laugh and jest, nor take any amusement. You are as sober as if you were in mourning for somebody.'

'Do you blame me for this, master? I shall never be able to please you in this respect, for I am fond neither of the bottle nor of the dance; I go neither to the tavern nor to balls; I know no funny stories nor nonsense. I care for nothing which might distract me from my duty.'

'You deserve to be held in high esteem for this, my boy, and I am not going to blame you for it. I mention it, because I believe that there is something on your mind. Perhaps you think that you are taking a great deal of trouble on behalf of other people, and are but poorly paid for it.'

'You are wrong in thinking so, Master Vertaud. My reward is as great as I could wish, and perhaps I could never have found elsewhere the high wages which you are willing to allow me, of your own free will, and without any urging from me. You have increased them, too, every year, and, on St John's day last, you fixed them at a hundred crowns, which is a very large price for you to pay. If you suffer any inconvenience from it, I assure you that I should gladly relinquish it.'

CHAPTER XIII

'COME, COME, François, we do not understand each other,' returned Master Jean Vertaud; 'and I do not know how to take you. You are no fool, and I think my hints have been broad enough; but you are so shy that I will help you out still further. Are not you in love with some girl about here?'

'No, master,' was the waif's honest answer.

'Truly?'

'I give you my word.'

'Don't you know one who might please you, if you were able to pay your court to her?'

'I have no desire to marry.'

'What an idea! You are too young to answer for that. What's your reason?'

'My reason? Do you really care to know, master?'

'Yes, because I feel an interest in you.'

'Then I will tell you; there is no occasion for me to hide it: I have never known father or mother. And there is something I have never told you; I was not obliged to do so; but if you had asked me, I should have told you the truth: I am a waif; I come from the foundling asylum.'

'Is it possible?' exclaimed Jean Vertaud, somewhat taken aback by this confession. 'I should never have thought it.'

'Why should you never have thought it? You do not answer, Master Vertaud. Very well, I shall answer for you. You saw that I was a good fellow, and you could not believe that a waif could be like that. It is true, then, that nobody has confidence in waifs, and that there is a prejudice against them. It is not just or humane; but since such a prejudice exists, everybody must conform to it, and the best people are not exempt, since you yourself—'

'No, no,' said Master Vertaud, with a revulsion of feeling, for he was a just man, and always ready to abjure a false notion. 'I do not wish to fail in justice, and if I forgot myself for a moment, you must forgive me, for that is all past now. So, you think you cannot marry, because you were born a waif?'

'Not at all, master; I do not consider that an obstacle. There are all sorts of women, and some of them are so kind-hearted that my misfortune might prove an inducement.'

'That is true,' cried Jean Vertaud. 'Women are better than we are. Yet,' he continued, with a laugh, 'a fine handsome fellow like you, in the flower of youth, and without any defect of body or mind, might very well add a zest to the pleasure of being charitable. But come, give me your reason.'

'Listen,' said François. 'I was taken from the asylum and nursed by a woman whom I never knew. At her death I was entrusted to another woman, who received me for the sake of the slender pittance granted by the government to those of my kind; but she was good to me, and when I was so unfortunate as to lose her, I should never have been comforted but for the help of another woman, who was the

best of the three, and whom I still love so much that I am
unwilling to live for any other woman but her. I have left
her, and perhaps I may never see her again, for she is well
off, and may never have need of me. Still, her husband has
had many secret expenses, and I have heard that he has
been ill since autumn, so it may be that he will die before
long, and leave her with more debts than property. If this
happened, master, I do not deny that I should return to the
place she lives in, and that my only care and desire would
be to assist her and her son, and keep them from poverty
by my toil. That is my reason for not undertaking any
engagement which would bind me elsewhere. You employ
me by the year, but if I married, I should be tied for life.
I should be assuming too many duties at once. If I had a
wife and children, it is not to be supposed that I could earn
enough bread for two families; neither is it to be supposed,
if, by extraordinary luck, I found a wife with some money
of her own, that I should have the right to deprive my
house of its comforts, to bestow them upon another's. Thus
I expect to remain a bachelor. I am young, and have time
enough before me; but if some fancy for a girl should enter
my head, I should try to get rid of it; because, do you see,
there is but one woman in the world for me, and that is my
mother Madeleine, who never despised me for being a waif,
but brought me up as her own child.'

'Is that it?' answered Jean Vertaud. 'My dear fellow, what
you tell me only increases my esteem for you. Nothing is so
ugly as ingratitude, and nothing so beautiful as the memory
of benefits received. I may have some good reasons for
showing you that you could many a young woman of the
same mind as yourself, who would join you in aiding your

old friend, but they are reasons which I must think over, and I must ask somebody else's opinion.'

No great cleverness was necessary to guess that Jean Vertaud, with his honest heart and sound judgement, had conceived of a marriage between his daughter and François. His daughter was comely, and though she was somewhat older than François, she had money enough to make up the difference. She was an only child, and a fine match, but up to this time, to her father's great vexation, she had refused to marry. He had observed lately that she thought a great deal of François, and had questioned her about him, but as she was a very reserved person, he had some difficulty in extorting any confession from her. Finally, without giving a positive answer, she consented to allow her father to sound François on the subject of marriage, and awaited the result with more uneasiness than she cared to show.

Jean Vertaud was disappointed that he had not a more satisfactory answer to carry to her; first, because he was so anxious to have her married, and next, because he could not wish for a better son-in-law than François. Besides the affection he felt for him, he saw clearly that the poor boy who had come to him was worth his weight in gold, on account of his intelligence, his quickness at his work, and his good conduct.

The young woman was a little pained to hear that François was a foundling. She was a trifle proud, but she made up her mind quickly, and her liking became more pronounced when she learned that François was backwards in love. Women go by contraries, and if François had schemed to obtain indulgence for the irregularity of his birth, he could have contrived no more artful device that that of showing a distaste towards marriage.

So it happened that Jean Vertaud's daughter decided in François's favour, that day, for the first time.

'Is that all?' said she to her father. 'Doesn't he think that we should have both the desire and the means to aid an old woman and find a situation for her son? He cannot have understood your hints, father, for if he knew it was a question of entering our family, he would have felt no such anxiety.'

That evening, when they were at work, Jeannette Vertaud said to François:

'I have always had a high opinion of you, François; but it is still higher now that my father has told me of your affection for the woman who brought you up, and for whom you wish to work all your life. It is right for you to feel so. I should like to know the woman, so that I might serve her in case of need, because you have always been so fond of her. She must be a fine woman.'

'Oh! Yes,' said François, who was pleased to talk of Madeleine. 'She is a woman with a good heart, a woman with a heart like yours.'

Jeannette Vertaud was delighted at this, and, thinking herself sure of what she wanted, went on:

'If she should turn out as unfortunate as you fear, I wish she could come and live with us. I should help you take care of her, for I suppose that she is no longer young. Is not she infirm?'

'Infirm? No,' said François. 'She is not old enough to be infirm.'

'Then is she still young?' asked Jeannette Vertaud, beginning to prick up her ears.

'Oh! No, she is not young,' answered François, simply. 'I do not remember how old she is now. She was a mother to me, and I never thought of her age.'

'Was she attractive?' asked Jeannette, after hesitating a moment before putting the question.

'Attractive?' said François, with some surprise. 'Do you mean to ask if she is a pretty woman? She is pretty enough for me just as she is; but to tell the truth, I never thought of that. What difference can it make in my affection for her? She might be as ugly as the devil, without my finding it out.'

'But cannot you tell me about how old she is?'

'Wait a minute. Her son was five years younger than I. Well! She is not old, but she is not very young; she is about like—'

'Like me?' said Jeannette, making a slight effort to laugh. 'In that case, if she becomes a widow, it will be too late for her to marry again, will it not?'

'That depends on circumstances,' replied François. 'If her husband has not wasted all the property, she would have plenty of suitors. There are fellows who would marry their great-aunts as wittingly as their great-nieces, for money.'

'Then you have no esteem for those who marry for money?'

'I could not do it,' answered François.

Simple-hearted as the waif was, he was no such simpleton as not to understand the insinuations which had been made him, and he did not speak without meaning. But Jeannette would not take the hint, and fell still deeper in love with him. She had had many admirers, without paying attention to any of them, and now the only one who pleased her, turned his back on her. Such is the logical temper of a woman's mind.

François observed during the following days that she had something on her mind, for she ate scarcely anything, and her eyes were always fixed on him, whenever she thought he was not looking. Her attachment pained him. He respected this good woman, and saw that the more indifferent he appeared, the more she cared about him; but he had no fancy for her, and if he had tried to cultivate such a feeling, it would have been the result of duty and principle rather than of spontaneous affection.

He reflected that he could not stay much longer with Jean Vertaud, because he knew that, sooner or later, such a condition of affairs must necessarily give rise to some unfortunate difference.

Just at this time, however, an incident befell which changed the current of his thoughts.

CHAPTER XIV

ONE MORNING the parish priest of Aigurande came strolling over to Jean Vertaud's mill, and wandered round the place for some time before espying François, whom he found at last in a corner of the garden. He assumed a very confidential air, and asked him if he were indeed François, surnamed Strawberry, a name that had been given him in the civil register – where he had been inscribed as a foundling – on account of a certain mark on his left arm. The priest then inquired concerning his exact age, the name of the woman who had nursed him, the places in which he had lived; in short, all that he knew of his birth and life.

François produced his papers, and the priest seemed to be entirely satisfied.

'Very well,' said he. 'You may come this evening or tomorrow morning to the parsonage; but you must not let anybody know what I am going to tell you, for I am forbidden to make it public, and it is a matter of conscience with me.'

When François went to the parsonage, the priest carefully shut the doors of the room, and drawing four little bits of thin paper from his desk, said:

'François Strawberry, there are four thousand francs that your mother sends you. I am forbidden to tell you her name, where she lives or whether she is alive or dead at the present moment. A pious thought has induced her to remember you, and it appears that she always intended to do so, since she knew where you were to be found, although you lived at such a distance. She knew that your character was good, and gives you enough to establish yourself with in life, on condition that for six months you never mention this gift, unless it be to the woman you want to marry. She enjoins me to consult with you on the investment or the safe deposit of this money, and begs me to lend my name, in case it is necessary, in order to keep the affair secret. I shall do as you like in this respect; but I am ordered to deliver you the money, only in exchange for your word of honour that you will neither say nor do anything that might divulge the secret. I know that I may count upon your good faith; will you pledge it to me?'

François gave his oath and left the money in the priest's charge, begging him to lay it out to the best advantage, for he knew this priest to be a good man; and some priests are like some women, either all good or all bad.

The waif returned home rather sad than glad. He thought of his mother, and would have been glad to give up the four thousand francs for the privilege of seeing and embracing her. He imagined, too, that perhaps she had just died, and that her gift was the result of one of those impulses which come to people at the point of death; and it made him still more melancholy to be unable to bear mourning for her and have masses said for her soul. Whether she were dead or alive, he prayed God to forgive her for forsaking her child, as her child forgave her with his whole heart, and prayed to be forgiven his sins in like manner.

He tried to appear the same as usual; but for more than a fortnight, he was so absorbed in a reverie at mealtimes that the attention of the Vertauds was excited.

'That young man does not confide in us,' observed the miller. 'He must be in love.'

'Perhaps it is with me,' thought the daughter, 'and he is too modest to confess it. He is afraid that I shall think him more attracted by my money than my person, so he is trying to prevent our guessing what is on his mind.'

Thereupon, she set to work to cure him of his shyness, and encouraged him so frankly and sweetly in her words and looks that he was a little touched in spite of his preoccupation.

Occasionally, he said to himself that he was rich enough to help Madeleine in case of need, and that he could well afford to marry a girl who laid no claim to his fortune. He was not in love with any woman, but he saw Jeannette Vertaud's good qualities, and was afraid of being hard-hearted if he did not respond to her advances. At times he pitied her, and was almost ready to console her.

But all at once, on a journey which he made to Crevant on his master's business, he met a forester from Presles, who told him of Cadet Blanchet's death, adding that he had left his affairs in great disorder, and that nobody knew whether his widow would be able to right them.

François had no cause to love or regret Master Blanchet, yet his heart was so tender that when he heard the news his eyes were moist and his head heavy, as if he were about to weep; he knew that Madeleine was weeping for her husband at that very moment, that she forgave him everything, and remembered only that he was the father of her child. The thought of Madeleine's grief awoke his own, and obliged him to weep with her over the sorrow which he was sure was hers.

His first impulse was to leap upon his horse and hasten to her side; but he reflected that it was his duty to ask permission of his master.

CHAPTER XV

'MASTER,' SAID HE to Jean Vertaud, 'I must leave you for a time; how long I cannot tell. I have something to attend to near my old home, and I request you to let me go with a good will; for, to tell the truth, if you refuse to give your permission, I shall not be able to obey you, but shall go in spite of you. Forgive me for stating the case plainly. I should be very sorry to vex you, and that is why I ask you, as a reward for all the services that I may have been able to render you, not to take my behaviour amiss, but to forgive the offence of which I am guilty, in leaving your work so suddenly. I may return at the end of a week, if I am not needed in the place where I am going; but I may not come back till late in the year, or not at all, for I am unwilling to deceive you. However, I shall do my best to come to your assistance if you need me, or if anything were to occur which you cannot manage without me. Before I go, I shall find you a good workman to take my place, and, if necessary, offer him as an inducement all that is due on my wages since St John's day last. Thus I can arrange matters without loss to you, and you must shake hands to wish me good luck, and to ease my mind of some of the regret I feel at parting with you.'

Jean Vertaud knew that the waif seldom asked for anything, but that when he did, his will was so firm that neither God nor the devil could bend it.

'Do as you please, my boy,' said he, shaking hands with him. 'I should not tell the truth if I said I did not care; but rather than have a quarrel with you, I should consent to anything.'

François spent the next day in looking up a servant to take his place in the mill, and he met with a zealous, upright man who was returning from the army, and was happy to find work and good wages under a good master; for Jean Vertaud was recognised as such, and was known never to have wronged anybody.

Before setting out, as he intended to do at daybreak the next day, François wished to take leave of Jeannette Vertaud at supper time. She was sitting at the barn door, saying that her head ached and that she could not eat. He observed that she had been weeping, and felt much troubled in mind. He did not know how to thank her for her kindness, and yet tell her that he was to leave her in spite of it. He sat down beside her on the stump of an alder tree, which happened to be there, and struggled to speak, without being able to think of a single word to say. She saw all this, without looking up, and pressed her handkerchief to her eyes. He made a motion to take her hand in his and comfort her, but drew back as it occurred to him that he could not conscientiously tell her what she wanted to hear. When poor Jeannette found that he remained silent, she was ashamed of her own sorrow, and, rising quietly without showing any bitterness of feeling, she went into the barn to weep unrestrained.

She lingered there a little while, in the hope that he would make up his mind to follow her and say a kind word, but he forbore, and went to his supper, which he ate in melancholy silence.

It would be false to say that he had felt nothing for Jeannette when he saw her in tears. His heart was a little fluttered, as he reflected how happy he might be with a person of so excellent a disposition, who was so fond of him, and who was not personally disagreeable to him. But he shook off all these ideas when it returned to his mind that Madeleine might stand in need of a friend, adviser and servant, and that when he was but a poor, forsaken child, wasted with fever, she had endured, worked and braved more for him than anybody else in the world.

'Come,' said he to himself, when he woke next morning before the dawn; 'you must not think of a love affair or your own happiness and tranquillity. You would gladly forget that you are a waif, and would throw your past to the winds, as so many others do, who seize the moment as it flies, without looking behind them. Yes, but think of Madeleine Blanchet, who entreats you not to forget her, but to remember what she did for you. Forward, then; and Jeannette, may God help you to a more gallant lover than your humble servant.'

Such were his reflections as he passed beneath the window of his kind mistress, and if the season had been propitious, he would have left a leaf or flower against her casement, in token of farewell; but it was the day after the feast of the Epiphany; the ground was covered with snow, and there was not a leaf on the trees nor a violet in the grass.

He thought of knotting into the corner of a white handkerchief the bean which he had won the evening before in the Twelfth Night cake, and of tying the handkerchief to the bars of Jeannette's window, to show her that he would have chosen her for his queen if she had deigned to appear at supper.

'A bean is a very little thing,' thought he, 'but it is a slight mark of courtesy and friendship, and will make my excuses for not having said goodbye to her.'

But a still, small voice within counselled him against making this offering, and pointed out to him that a man should not follow the example of those young girls who try to make men love, remember and regret them when they have not the slightest idea of giving anything in return.

'No, no, François,' said he, putting back his pledge into his pocket, and hastening his step; 'a man's will must be firm, and he must allow himself to be forgotten when he has made up his mind to forget himself.'

Thereupon, he strode rapidly away, and before he had gone two gunshots from Jean Vertaud's mill he fancied that he saw Madeleine's image before him, and heard a faint little voice calling to him for help. This dream drew him on, and he seemed to see already the great ash tree, the fountain, the meadow of the Blanchets, the mill-dam, the little bridge and Jeannie running to meet him; and in the midst of all this, the memory of Jeannette Vertaud was powerless to hold him back an inch.

He walked so fast that he felt neither cold nor hunger nor thirst, nor did he stop to take breath till he left the high road and reached the cross of Plessys, which stands at the beginning of the path which leads to Presles.

When there, he flung himself on his knees and kissed the wood of the cross with the ardour of a good Christian who meets again with a good friend. Then he began to descend the great track, which is like a road, except that it is as broad as a field. It is the finest common in the world, and is blessed with a beautiful view, fresh air and extended horizon. It slopes so rapidly that in frosty weather a man could go post-haste even in an ox-cart and take an unexpected plunge in the river, which runs silently below.

François mistrusted this; he took off his sabots more than once, and reached the bridge without a tumble. He passed by Montipouret on the left, not without sending a loving salute to the tall old clock tower, which is everybody's friend; for it is the first to greet the eyes of those who are returning home, and shows them the right road, if they have gone astray.

As to the roads, I have no fault to find with them in summer time, when they are green, smiling and pleasant to look upon. You may walk through some of them with no fear of a sunstroke; but those are the most treacherous of all, because they may lead you to Rome, when you think you are going to Angibault. Happily, the good clock tower of Montipouret is not chary of showing itself, and through every dealing you may catch a glimpse of its glittering steeple, that tells you whether you are going north or north-west.

The waif, however, needed no such beacon to guide him. He was so familiar with all the wooded paths and byways, all the shady lanes, all the hunters' trails, and even the very hedgerows along the roads, that in the middle of the night he could take the shortest cut, and go as straight as a pigeon flies through the sky.

It was towards noon when he first caught sight of the mill of Cormouer through the leafless branches, and he was happy to see curling up from the roof a faint blue smoke, which assured him that the house was not abandoned to the rats.

For greater speed he crossed the upper part of the Blanchet meadow, and thus did not pass close by the fountain; but as the trees and bushes were stripped of their leaves, he could still see sparkling in the sunlight the open water, which never freezes, because it bubbles up from a spring. The approach to the mill, on the contrary, was icy and so slippery that much caution was required to step safely over the stones, and along the bank of the river. He saw the old mill wheel, black with age and damp, covered with long icicles, sharp as needles, that hung from the bars.

Many trees were missing around the house, and the place was much changed. Cadet Blanchet's debts had called the axe into play, and here and there were to be seen the stumps of great alders, freshly cut, as red as blood. The house seemed to be in bad repair; the roof was ill-protected, and the oven had cracked half open by the action of the frost.

What was still more melancholy was that there was no sound to be heard of man or beast; only a brindled black-and-white dog, a poor country mongrel, jumped up from the doorstep and ran barking towards François; then he suddenly ceased, and came crawling up to him and lay at his feet.

'Is it you, Labriche, and do you know me?' said François. 'I did not recognise you, for you are so old and miserable; your ribs stick out, and your whiskers are quite white.'

François talked thus to the dog, because he was distressed, and wanted to gain a little time before entering the house. He had been in great haste up to this moment, but now he was alarmed, because he feared that he should never see Madeleine again, that she might be absent or dead instead of her husband, or that the report of the miller's death might prove false; in short, he was a prey to all those fancies which beset the mind of a man who has just reached the goal of all his desires.

CHAPTER XVI

FINALLY FRANÇOIS drew the latch of the door, and beheld, instead of Madeleine, a lovely young girl, rosy as a May morning, and lively as a linnet. She said to him, with an engaging manner: 'What is it you want, young man?'

Though she was so fair to see, François did not waste time in looking at her, but cast his eyes round the room in search of Madeleine. He saw nothing but the closed curtains of her bed, and he was sure that she was in it. He did not wait to answer the pretty girl, who was Mariette Blanchet, the miller's youngest sister, but without a word walked up to the yellow bed and pulled the curtains noiselessly aside; there he saw Madeleine Blanchet lying asleep, pale and wasted with fever.

He looked at her long and fixedly, without moving or speaking; and in spite of his grief at her illness, and his fear of her dying, he was yet happy to have her face before him, and to be able to say: 'I see Madeleine.'

Mariette Blanchet pushed him gently away from the bed, drew the curtains together, and beckoned to him to follow her to the fireside.

'Now, young man,' said she, 'who are you, and what do you want? I do not know you, and you are a stranger in the neighbourhood. Tell me how I may oblige you.'

François did not listen to her, and instead of answering her, he began to ask questions about how long Madame Blanchet had been ill, whether she were in any danger, and whether she were well cared for.

Mariette answered that Madeleine had been ill since her husband's death, because she had overexerted herself in nursing him, and watching at his bedside, day and night; that they had not as yet sent for the doctor, but that they would do so in case she was worse; and as to her being well cared for, Mariette declared that she knew her duty and did not spare herself.

At these words, the waif looked the girl full in the face, and had no need to ask her name, for besides knowing that soon after he had left the mill, Master Blanchet had placed his sister in his wife's charge, he detected in the pretty face of this pretty girl a striking resemblance to the sinister face of the dead miller. There are many fine and delicate faces which have an inexplicable likeness to ugly ones; and though Mariette Blanchet's appearance was as charming as that of her brother had been disagreeable, she still had an unmistakable family look. Only the miller's expression had been surly and irascible, while Mariette's was mocking rather than resentful, and fearless instead of threatening.

So it was that François was neither altogether disturbed nor altogether at ease concerning the attention Madeleine might receive from this young girl. Her cap was of fine linen, neatly folded and pinned; her hair, which she wore somewhat after the fashion of town-bred girls, was very lustrous, and carefully combed and parted; and both her hands and her apron were very white for a sick nurse. In short, she was much too young, fresh, and gay to spend the day and night in helping a person who was unable to help herself.

François asked no more questions, but sat down in the chimney corner, determined not to leave the place until he saw whether his dear Madeleine's illness turned for the better or worse.

Mariette was astonished to see him take possession of the fire so cavalierly, just as if he were in his own house. He stared into the blaze, and as he seemed in no humour for talking, she dared inquire no further who he was and what was his business. After a moment, Catherine, who had been the house servant for eighteen or twenty years, came into the room. She paid no attention to him, but approached the bed of her mistress, looked at her cautiously and then turned to the fireplace, to see after the potion which Mariette was concocting. Her behaviour showed an intense interest for Madeleine, and François, who took the truth of the matter in a throb, was on the point of addressing her with a friendly greeting; but—

'But,' said the priest's servant, interrupting the hemp-dresser, 'you are using an unsuitable word. A *throb* does not express a moment, or a minute.'

'I tell you,' retorted the hemp-dresser, 'that a moment means nothing at all, and a minute is longer than it takes for an idea to rush into the head. I do not know how many millions of things you can think of in a minute, whereas you only need a throb of time to see and hear some one thing that is happening. I will say a little throb, if you please.'

'But a throb of time!' objected the old purist.

'Ah! A throb of time! Does that worry you, Mother Monique? Does not everything go by throbs? Does not the sun, when you see it rising in the clouds of flames, and it makes your eyes blink to look at it? And the blood that beats in your veins; the church clock that sifts your time particle by particle, as a bolting-machine does the grain; your rosary when you tell it; your heart when the priest is delayed in coming home; the rain falling drop by drop, and the earth that turns round, as they say, like a mill wheel? Neither you nor I feel the motion – the machine is too well oiled for that; but there must be some throbbing about it, since it accomplishes its period in twenty-four hours. As to that, too, we use the word *period* when we speak of a certain length of time. So I say a *throb*, and I shall not unsay it. Do not interrupt me any more, unless you wish to tell the story.'

'No, no; your machine is too well oiled, too,' answered the old woman. 'Now let your tongue throb a little longer.'

CHAPTER XVII

I WAS SAYING THAT François was tempted to speak to big old Catherine, and make himself known to her; but as in the same throb of time he was on the point of crying, he did not wish to behave like a fool, and did not even raise his head. As Catherine stooped over the ashes, she caught sight of his long legs and drew back in alarm.

'What is all that?' whispered she to Mariette in the other corner of the room. 'Where does that man come from?'

'Do you ask me?' said the girl. 'How should I know? I never saw him before. He came in here, as if he were at an inn, without a good-morning or good-evening. He asked after the health of my sister-in-law as if he were a near relation, or her heir; and there he is sitting by the fire, as you see. You may speak to him, for I do not care to do so. He may be a disreputable person.'

'What? Do you think he is crazy? He does not look wicked, as far as I can see, for he seems to be hiding his face.'

'Suppose he has come for some bad purpose?'

'Do not be afraid, Mariette, for I am near to keep him in check. If he alarms you, I shall pour a kettle of boiling water over his legs, and throw an andiron at his head.'

While they were chattering thus, François was thinking of Madeleine.

'That poor dear woman,' said he to himself, 'who has never had anything but vexation and unkindness from her husband, is now lying ill because she nursed and helped him to the end. Here is this young girl, who was the miller's pet sister, as I have heard say, and her face bears no traces of sorrow. She shows no signs of fatigue or tears, for her eyes are as dear and bright as the sun.'

He could not help looking at her from under the brim of his hat, for never until then had he seen such fresh and joyous beauty. Still, though his eyes were charmed, his heart remained untouched.

'Come,' continued Catherine, in a whisper to her young mistress, 'I am going to speak to him. I must find out his business here.'

'Speak to him politely,' said Mariette. 'We must not irritate him; we are all alone in the house, and Jeannie may be too far away to hear our cries.'

'Jeannie!' exclaimed François, who caught nothing from all their prattle, except the name of his old friend. 'Where is Jeannie, and why don't I see him? Has he grown tall, strong and handsome?'

'There,' thought Catherine, 'he asks this because he has some evil intention. Who is the man, for Heaven's sake? I know neither his voice nor his figure; I must satisfy myself and look at his face.'

She was strong as a labourer and bold as a soldier, and would not have quailed before the devil himself, so she stalked up to François, determined either to make him take off his hat, or to knock it off herself, so that she might see whether he were a monster or a Christian man. She approached the waif, without suspecting that it was he; for being as little given to thinking of the past as of the future, she had long forgotten all about François, and, moreover, he had improved so much and was now such a handsome fellow that she might well have looked at him several times before recalling him to mind; but just as she was about to accost him rather roughly, Madeleine awoke, and called Catherine, saying in a faint, almost inaudible voice that she was burning with thirst.

François sprang up, and would have been the first to reach her but for the fear of exciting her too much, which held him back. He quickly handed the draught to Catherine, who hastened with it to her mistress, forgetting everything for the moment but the sick woman's condition.

Mariette, too, did her share, by raising Madeleine in her arms, to help her drink, and this was no hard task, for Madeleine was so thin and wasted that it was heartbreaking to see her.

'How do you feel, sister?' asked Mariette.

'Very well, my child,' answered Madeleine, in the tone of one about to die. She never complained, to avoid distressing the others.

'That is not Jeannie over there,' she said, as she caught sight of the waif. 'Am I dreaming, my child, or who is that tall man standing by the fire?'

Catherine answered: 'We do not know, dear mistress; he says nothing, and behaves like an idiot.'

The waif, at this moment, made a little motion to go towards Madeleine, but restrained himself, for though he was dying to speak to her, he was afraid of taking her by surprise. Catherine now saw his face, but he had changed so much in the past three years that she did not recognise him, and thinking that Madeleine was frightened, she said:

'Do not worry, dear mistress; I was just going to turn him out, when you called me.'

'Don't turn him out,' said Madeleine, in a stronger voice, pulling aside the curtain of her bed; 'I know him, and he has done right in coming to see me. Come nearer, my son; I have been praying God every day to permit me the grace of giving you my blessing.'

The waif ran to her, and threw himself on his knees beside her bed, shedding tears of joy and sorrow that nearly suffocated him. Madeleine touched his hands, and then his head; and said, as she kissed him:

'Call Jeannie; Catherine, call Jeannie, that he may share this happiness with us. Ah! I thank God, François, and I am ready to die now, if such is his will, for both my children are grown, and I may bid them farewell in peace.'

CHAPTER XVIII

C ATHERINE RUSHED OFF in pursuit of Jeannie, and
Mariette was so anxious to know what it all meant
that she followed to ask questions. François was left
alone with Madeleine, who kissed him again, and burst into
tears; then she closed her eyes, looking still more weak and
exhausted than she had been before. François saw that she had
fainted, and knew not how to revive her; he was beside himself,
and could only hold her in his arms, calling her his dear mother,
his dearest friend, and imploring her, as if it lay within her
power, not to die so soon, without hearing what he had to say.

So, by his tender words, devoted care and fond endearments,
he restored her to consciousness, and she began again to see
and hear him. He told her that he had guessed she needed
him, that he had left all, and had come to stay as long as she
wanted him, and that, if she would take him for her servant,
he would ask nothing but the pleasure of working for her, and
the solace of spending his life in her service.

'Do not answer,' he continued; 'do not speak, my dear
mother; you are too weak, and must not say a word. Only look
at me, if you are pleased to see me again, and I shall understand that you accept my friendship and help.'

Madeleine looked at him so serenely, and was so much comforted by what he said, that they were contented and happy together, notwithstanding the misfortune of her illness.

Jeannie, who came in answer to Catherine's loud cries, arrived to take his share of their joy. He had grown into a handsome boy between fourteen and fifteen, and though not strong, he was delightfully active, and so well brought up that he was always friendly and polite.

'Oh! How glad I am to see you like this, Jeannie,' said François. 'You are not very tall and strong, but I am satisfied, because I think you will need my help in climbing trees and crossing the river. I see that you are delicate, though you are not ill, isn't it so? Well, you shall be my child, still a little while longer, if you do not mind. Yes, yes; you will find me necessary to you; and you will make me carry out your wishes, just as it was long ago.'

'Yes,' said Jeannie; 'my four hundred wishes, as you used to call them.'

'Oho! What a good memory you have! How nice it was of you, Jeannie, not to forget François! But have we still four hundred wishes a day?'

'Oh, no,' said Madeleine; 'he has grown very reasonable; he has no more than two hundred now.'

'No more nor less?' asked François.

'Just as you like,' answered Jeannie; 'since my darling mother is beginning to smile again, I am ready to agree to anything. I am even willing to say that I wish more than five hundred times a day to see her well again.'

'That is right, Jeannie,' said François. 'See how nicely he talks! Yes, my boy, God will grant those five hundred wishes of yours. We shall take such good care of your darling mother, and shall cheer and gladden her little by little, until she forgets her weariness.'

Catherine stood at the threshold, and was most anxious to come in, to see and speak to François, but Mariette held her by the sleeve, and would not leave off asking questions.

'What,' said she, 'is he a foundling? He looks so respectable.'

She was looking through the crack in the door, which she held ajar.

'How comes it that he and Madeleine are such friends?'

'I tell you that she brought him up, and that he was always a very good boy.'

'She has never spoken of him to me, nor have you.'

'Oh, goodness, no! I never thought of it; he was away; and I almost forgot him; then, I knew, too, that my mistress had been in trouble on his account, and I did not wish to recall it to her mind.'

'Trouble! What kind of trouble?'

'Oh! Because she was so fond of him; she could not help liking him, he had such a good heart, poor child. Your brother would not allow him in the house, and you know your brother was not always very gentle!'

'We must not say that, now that he is dead, Catherine.'

'Yes, yes; you are right; I was not thinking. Dear me, how short my memory is! And yet it is only two weeks since he died! But let me go in, my young lady; I want to give the boy some dinner, for I think he must be hungry.'

She shook herself loose, ran up to François and kissed him. He was so handsome that she no longer remembered having once said that she would rather kiss her sabot than a foundling.

'Oh, poor François,' said she, 'how glad I am to see you! I was afraid that you would never come back. See, my dear mistress, how changed he is! I wonder that you were able to recognise him at once. If you had not told me who he was, I should not have known him for ages. How handsome he is, isn't he? His beard is beginning to grow; yes, you cannot see it much, but you can feel it. It did not prick when you went away, François, but now it pricks a little. And how strong you are, my friend! What hands and arms and legs you have! A workman like you is worth three. What wages are you getting now?'

Madeleine laughed softly to see Catherine so pleased with François, and was overjoyed that he was so strong and vigorous. She wished that her Jeannie might grow up to be like him. Mariette was ashamed to have Catherine look so boldly in a man's face, and blushed involuntarily. But the more she tried not to look at him, the more her eyes strayed towards him; she saw that Catherine was right; he was certainly remarkably handsome, tall and erect as a young oak.

Then, without stopping to think, she began to serve him very politely, pouring out the best wine of that year's vintage, and recalling his attention when it wandered to Madeleine and Jeannie, and he forgot to eat.

'You must eat more,' said she; 'you scarcely take anything. You should have more appetite after so long a journey.'

'Pay no attention to me, young lady,' answered François, at last; 'I am too happy to be here to care about eating and drinking. Come now,' continued he, turning to Catherine, when the room was put to rights, 'show me round the mill and the house, for everything looks neglected, and I want to talk to you about it.'

When they were outside, he questioned her intelligently on the state of things, with the air of a man determined to know the whole truth.

'Oh, François,' said Catherine, bursting into tears, 'everything is going to grief, and if nobody comes to the assistance of my poor mistress, I believe that wicked woman will turn her out of doors, and make her spend all she owns in lawsuits.'

'Do not cry,' said François, 'for if you do, I cannot understand what you say; try to speak more clearly. What wicked woman do you mean? Is it Sévère?'

'Oh! Yes, to be sure. She is not content with having ruined our master, but now lays claim to everything he left. She is trying to prosecute us in fifty different ways; she says that Cadet Blanchet gave her promissory notes, and that even if she sold everything over our heads she would not be paid. She sends us bailiffs every day, and the expenses are already considerable. Our mistress has paid all she could, in trying to pacify her, and I am very much afraid that she will die of this worry, on top of all the fatigue she underwent during her husband's illness. At this rate, we shall soon be without food and fire. The servant of the mill has left us, because he was owed two years' wages, and could not be paid. The mill has stopped running, and if this goes on, we shall lose our customers. The horses and crops have been attached, and are to be sold; the trees are to be cut down. Oh, François, it is ruin!'

Her tears began to flow afresh.

'And how about you, Catherine?' asked François. 'Are you a creditor, too? Have your wages been paid?'

'I, a creditor?' said Catherine, changing her wail into a roar. 'Never, never! It is nobody's business whether my wages are paid or not!'

'Good for you, Catherine; you show the right spirit!' said François. 'Keep on taking care of your mistress, and do not bother about the rest. I have earned a little money in my last place, and I have enough with me to save the horses, the crops and the trees. I am going to pay a little visit to the mill, and if I find it in disorder, I shall not need a wheelwright to set it going again. Jeannie is as swift as a little bird, and he must set out immediately and run all day, and then begin again tomorrow morning, so as to let all the customers know that the mill is creaking like ten thousand devils, and that the miller is waiting to grind the corn.'

'Shall we send for a doctor for our mistress?'

'I have been thinking about it; but I am going to wait and watch her all day before making up my mind.

'Do you see, Catherine, I believe that doctors are useful when the sick cannot do without them; but if the disease is not violent, it is easier to recover with God's help than with their drugs: not taking into consideration that the mere presence of a doctor, which cures the rich, often kills the poor. He cheers and amuses those who live in luxury, but he scares and oppresses those who never see him except in the day of danger. It seems to me that Madame Blanchet will recover very soon, if her affairs are straightened.

'And before we finish this conversation, Catherine, tell me one thing more; I ask the truth of you, and you must not scruple to tell it to me. It will go no further; I have not changed, and if you remember me, you must know that a secret is safe in the waif's bosom.'

'Yes, yes, I know,' said Catherine; 'but why do you consider yourself a waif? Nobody will call you any more by that name, for you do not deserve it, François.'

'Never mind that. I shall always be what I am, and I am not in the habit of plaguing myself about it. Tell me what you think of your young mistress, Mariette Blanchet.'

'Oh, she! She is a pretty girl. Have you already taken it into your head to marry her? She has some money of her own; her brother could not touch her property, because she was a minor, and unless you have fallen heir to an estate, Master François—'

'Waifs never inherit anything,' said François, 'and as to marrying, I have as much time to think of it as the chestnut in the fire. What I want to hear from you is whether this girl is better than her brother, and whether she will prove a source of comfort or trouble to Madeleine, if she stays on here.'

'Heaven knows,' said Catherine, 'for I do not. Until now, she has been thoughtless and innocent enough. She likes dress, caps trimmed with lace, and dancing. She is not very selfish, but she has been so well-treated and spoiled by Madeleine that she has never had occasion to show whether she could bite or not. She has never had anything to suffer, so we cannot tell what she may be.'

'Was she very fond of her brother?'

'Not very, except when he took her to balls, and our mistress tried to convince him that it was not proper to take a respectable girl in Sévère's company. Then the little girl, who thought of nothing but her own pleasure, overwhelmed her brother with attentions, and turned up her nose at Madeleine, who was obliged to yield. So Mariette does not dislike Sévère as much as I should wish to have her, but I cannot say that she is not good-natured and nice to her sister-in-law.'

'That will do, Catherine; I ask nothing further. Only I forbid you to tell the young girl anything of what we have been talking about.'

François accomplished successfully all that he had promised Catherine. By evening, owing to Jeannie's diligence, corn arrived to be ground, and the mill too was in working order; the ice was broken and melted about the wheel, the machinery was oiled and the woodwork repaired, wherever it was broken. The energetic François worked till two in the morning, and at four he was up again. He stepped noiselessly into Madeleine's room, and finding the faithful Catherine on guard, he asked how the patient was. She had slept well, happy in the arrival of her beloved servant, and in the efficient aid he brought. Catherine refused to leave her mistress before Mariette appeared, and François asked at what hour the beauty of Cormouer was in the habit of rising.

'Not before daylight,' said Catherine.

'What? Then you have two more hours to wait, and you will get no sleep at all.'

'I sleep a little in the daytime, in my chair, or on the straw in the barn, while the cows are feeding.'

'Very well, go to bed now,' said François, 'and I shall wait here to show the young lady that some people go to bed later than she, and get up earlier in the morning. I shall busy myself with examining the miller's papers and those which the bailiffs have brought since his death. Where are they?'

'There, in Madeleine's chest,' said Catherine. 'I am going to light the lamp, François. Come, courage, and try your best to make things straight, as you seem to understand law-papers.'

She went to bed, obeying the commands of the waif as if he were the master of the house; for true it is that he who has a good head and good heart rules by his own right.

CHAPTER XIX

B EFORE SETTING TO WORK, François, as soon
as he was left alone with Madeleine and Jeannie
(for the young child always slept in the room with
his mother), went to take a look at the sleeping woman,
and thought her appearance better than when he had first
arrived. He was happy to think that she would have no need
of a doctor, and that he alone, by the comfort he brought,
would preserve her health and fortune.

He began to look over the papers, and was soon fully
acquainted with Sévère's claims and the amount of property
that Madeleine still possessed with which to satisfy them.
Besides all that Sévère had already made Cadet Blanchet
squander upon her, she declared that she was still a creditor for
two hundred pistoles, and Madeleine had scarcely anything
of her own property left in addition to the inheritance that
Blanchet had bequeathed to Jeannie — an inheritance now
reduced to the mill and its immediate belongings — that is,
the courtyard, the meadow, the outbuildings, the garden,
the hemp-field and a bit of planted ground; for the broad
fields and acres had melted like snow in the hands of Cadet
Blanchet.

'Thank God!' thought François. 'I have four hundred pistoles in the charge of the priest of Aigurande, and in case I can do no better, Madeleine can still have her house, the income of her mill and what remains of her dowry. But I think we can get off more easily than that. In the first place, I must find out whether the notes signed by Blanchet to Sévère were not extorted by stratagem and undue influence, and then I must do a stroke of business on the lands he sold. I understand how such affairs are managed, and knowing the names of the purchasers, I will put my hand in the fire if I cannot bring this to a successful issue.'

The fact was that Blanchet, two or three years before his death, straightened for money and over head and ears in debt to Sévère, had sold his land at a low price to whomsoever wanted to buy, and turned all his claims for it over to Sévère, thus expecting to rid himself of her and of her comrades who had helped her to ruin him. But, as usually happens in such sales, almost all those who hastened to buy, attracted by the sweet fragrance of the fertile lands, had not a penny with which to pay for them, and only discharged the interest with great difficulty. This state of things might last from ten to twenty years; it was an investment for Sévère and her friends, but a bad investment, and she complained loudly of Cadet Blanchet's rashness, and feared that she would never be paid. So she said, at least; but the speculation was really a reasonably good one. The peasant, even if he has to lie on straw, pays his interest, so unwilling is he to let go the bit of land he holds, which his creditor may seize if he is not satisfied.

We all know this, my good friends, and we often try to grow rich the wrong way, by buying fine property at a low price.

However low it may be, it is always too high for us. Our covetousness is more capacious than our purse, and we take no end of trouble to cultivate a field the produce of which does not cover half the interest exacted by the seller.

When we have delved and sweated all our poor lives, we find ourselves ruined, and the earth alone is enriched by our pains and toil. Just as we have doubled its value, we are obliged to sell it. If we could sell it advantageously, we should be safe; but this is never possible. We have been so drained by the interest we have had to pay that we must sell in haste, and for anything we can get. If we rebel, we are forced into it by the law courts, and the man who first sold the land gets back his property in the condition in which he finds if; that means that for long years he has placed his land in our hands at eight or ten per cent, and when he resumes possession of it, it is by our labours, twice as valuable, in consequence of a careful cultivation which has lost him neither trouble nor expense, and also by the lapse of time which always increases the value of property. Thus we poor little minnows are to be continually devoured by the big fish which pursue us; punished always for our love of gain, and just as foolish as we were before.

Sévère's money was thus profitably invested in a mortgage at a high interest, but at the same time she had a firm hold of Cadet Blanchet's estate, because she had managed him so cleverly that he had pledged himself for the purchasers of his land, and had gone surety for their payment.

François saw all this intrigue, and meditated some possible means of buying back the land at a low price, without ruining anybody, and of playing a tine trick upon Sévère and her clan, by causing the failure of their speculation.

It was no easy matter. He had enough money to buy back almost everything at the price of the original sale, and neither Sévère nor anybody else could refuse to be reimbursed. The buyers would find it to their profit to sell again in all haste, in order to escape approaching ruin; for I tell you all, young and old, if you buy land on credit, you take out a patent for beggary in your old age. It is useless for me to tell you this, for you will have the buying mania no whit the less. Nobody can see a ploughed furrow smoking in the sun without being in a fever to possess it, and it was the peasant's mad fever to hold on to his own piece of soil that caused Francois's uneasiness.

Do you know what the soil is, my children? Once upon a time, everybody in our parishes was talking about it. They said that the old nobles had attached us to the soil to make us drudge and die, but the Revolution had burst our bonds, and that we no longer drew our master's cart like oxen. The truth is that we have bound ourselves to our own acres, and we drudge and die no less than before.

The city people tell us that our only remedy would be to have no wants or desires. Only last Sunday, I answered a man who was preaching this doctrine very eloquently, that if we poor peasants could only be sensible enough never to eat or sleep, to work all the time, and to drink nothing but fresh, clear water, provided the frogs had no objection, we might succeed in saving a goodly hoard, and in receiving a shower of compliments for our wisdom and discretion.

Following this same train of thought, François cudgelled his brains to find some means of inducing the purchasers of the land to sell it back again. He finally hit upon the plan of whispering in their ears the little falsehood, that though Sévère had the reputation of being fabulously rich, she had really as many debts as a sieve has holes, and that some fine morning her creditors would lay hands upon all her claims, as well as upon all her property. He meant to tell them this confidentially, and when they were thoroughly alarmed, he expected to buy back Madeleine Blanchet's lands at the original price, with his own money.

He scrupled, however, to tell this untruth, until it occurred to him that he could give a small bonus to all the poor purchasers, to make them amends for the interest they had already paid. In this manner Madeleine could be restored to her rights and possessions without loss or injury to the purchasers.

The discredit in which Sévère would be involved by his plan caused him no scruple whatever. It is right for the hen to pull out a feather from the cruel bird that has plucked her chickens.

When François had reached this conclusion, Jeannie awoke, and arose softly, to avoid disturbing his mother's slumbers; then, after a good-morning to François, he lost no time in going off to announce to the rest of their customers that the mill was in good order, and that a strong young miller stood in readiness to grind the corn.

CHAPTER XX

I T WAS ALREADY broad daylight when Mariette Blanchet emerged from her nest, carefully attired in her mourning, which was so very black and so very white that she looked as spick and span as a little magpie. The poor child had one great care, and that was that her mourning would long prevent her going to dances, and that all her admirers would be missing her. Her heart was so good that she pitied them greatly.

'How is this?' said she, as she saw François arranging the papers in Madeleine's room. 'You attend to everything here, Master Miller! You make flour, you settle the business, you mix the medicines; soon we shall see you sewing and spinning.'

'And you, my young lady,' said François, who saw that she regarded him favourably, although she slashed him with her tongue, 'I have never as yet seen you sewing or spinning; I think we shall soon find you sleeping till noon, and it will do you good, and keep your cheeks rosy!'

'Oho! Master François, you are already beginning to tell me truths about myself. You had better take care of that little game; I can tell you something in return.'

'I await your pleasure, my young lady.'

'It will soon come; do not be afraid, Master Miller. Have the kindness to tell me where Catherine is, and why you are here watching beside our patient. Should you like a hood and gown?'

'Are you going to ask, in your turn, for a cap and blouse, so that you may go to the mill? As I see you do no woman's work, which would be nursing your sister for a little while, I suppose you would like to sift out the chaff, and turn the grindstone. At your service. Let us change clothes.'

'It looks as if you were trying to give me a lesson.'

'No; you gave me one first, and I am only returning, out of politeness, what you lent me.'

'Good! You like to laugh and tease, but you have chosen the wrong time. We are not merry here, and it is only a short time ago that we had to go to the graveyard. If you chatter so much, you will prevent my sister-in-law from getting the sleep she needs so greatly.'

'On that very account, you should not raise your voice so much, my young lady; for I am speaking very low, and you are not speaking, just now, as you should in a sickroom.'

'Enough, if you please, Master François,' said Mariette, lowering her tone, and flushing angrily. 'Be so good as to see if Catherine is at hand, and tell me why she leaves my sister-in-law in your charge.'

'Excuse me, my young lady,' said François, with no sign of temper. 'She could not leave her in your charge, because you are too fond of sleeping, so she was obliged to entrust her to mine. I shall not call her, because the poor woman is jaded with fatigue. Without meaning to offend you, I must say that she has been sitting up every night for two weeks. I sent her off to bed, and, until noon, I mean to do her work and mine too, for it is only right for us all to help one another.'

'Listen, Master François,' said the young girl, with a sudden change of tone; 'you appear to hint that I think only of myself and leave all the work to others. Perhaps I should have sat up in my turn, if Catherine had told me that she was tired; but she insisted that she was not at all tired, and I did not understand that my sister was so seriously ill. You think that I have a bad heart, but I cannot imagine where you have learned it. You never knew me before yesterday, and we are not, as yet, intimate enough for you to scold me as you do. You behave exactly as if you were the head of the family, and yet—'

'Come, out with it, beautiful Mariette, say what you have on the tip of your tongue. And yet I was taken in and brought up out of charity, is not it so? And I cannot belong to the family, because I have no family; I have no right to it, as I am a foundling! Is that all you wanted to say?'

As François gave Mariette this straightforward answer, he looked at her in a way that made her blush up to the roots of her hair, for she saw that his expression was that of a stem and serious person, although he appeared so serene and gentle that it was impossible to irritate him, or to make him think or say anything unjust.

The poor child, who was ordinarily so ready with her tongue, was overawed for a moment, but although she was a little frightened, she still felt a desire to please this handsome fellow, who spoke so decidedly and looked her so frankly in the eyes. She was so confused and embarrassed that it was with difficulty she restrained her tears, and she turned her face quickly the other way, to hide her emotion.

He observed it, however, and said very kindly: 'I am not angry, Mariette, and you have no cause to be, on your part. I think no ill of you; I see only that you are young, that there is misfortune in the house, and that you are thoughtless. I must tell you what I think about it.'

'What do you think about it?' asked she. 'Tell me at once, that I may know whether you are my friend or my enemy.'

'I think that you are not fond of the care and pains people take for those whom they love, who are in trouble. You like to have your time to yourself, to turn everything into sport, to think about your dress, your lovers and your marriage by and by, and you do not mind having others do your share. If you have any heart, my pretty child, if you really love your sister-in-law, and your dear little nephew, and even the poor, faithful servant who is capable of dying in harness like a good horse, you must wake up a little earlier in the morning, you must care for Madeleine, comfort Jeannie, relieve Catherine, and, above all, shut your ears to the enemy of the family, Madame Sévère, who is, I assure you, a very bad woman. Now you know what I think, neither more nor less.'

'I am glad to hear it,' said Mariette, rather dryly; 'and now please tell me by what right you wish to make me think as you do.'

'Oh! This is the way you take it, is it?' answered François. 'My right is the waif's right, and to tell you the whole truth, the right of the child who was taken in and brought up by Madame Blanchet; for this, it is my duty to love her as my mother, and my right to try to requite her for her kindness.'

'I have no fault to find,' returned Mariette, 'and I see that I cannot do better than give you my respect at once, and my friendship as time goes on.'

'I like that,' said François; 'shake hands with me on it.'

He strode towards her, holding out his great hand, without the slightest awkwardness; but the little Mariette was suddenly stung by the fly of coquetry, and, withdrawing her hand, she announced that it was not proper to shake hands so familiarly with a young man.

François laughed and left her, seeing plainly that she was not frank, and that her first object was to entangle him in a flirtation.

'Now, my pretty girl,' thought he, 'you are much mistaken in me, and we shall not be friends in the way you mean.'

He went up to Madeleine, who had just waked, and who said to him, taking both his hands in hers:

'I have slept well, my son, and God is gracious to let me see your face first of all, on waking. How is it that Jeannie is not with you?'

Then, after hearing his explanation, she spoke some kind words to Mariette, telling the young girl how sorry she was to have her sit up all night, and assuring her that she needed no such great care. Mariette expected François to say that she had risen very late; but François said nothing and left her alone with Madeleine, who had no more fever and wanted to try to get up.

After three days, she was so much better that she was able to talk over business affairs with François.

'You may put yourself at ease, my dear mother,' said he. 'I sharpened my wits when I was away from here, and I understand business pretty well. I mean to see you through these straits, and I shall succeed. Let me have my way; please do not contradict anything I say, and sign all the papers I shall bring you. Now, that my mind is at ease on the score of your health, I am going to town to consult some lawyers. It is market day, and I shall find some people there whom I want to see, and I do not think my time will be wasted.'

He did as he said; and after receiving instructions and advice from the lawyers, he saw clearly that the last promissory notes which Blanchet had given Sévère would be a good subject for a lawsuit; for he had signed them when he was beside himself with drink, fever and infatuation. Sévère believed that Madeleine would not dare to go to law, on account of the expense. François was unwilling to advise Madame Blanchet to embark in a lawsuit, but he thought there was a reasonable chance of bringing the matter to an amicable close, if he began by putting a bold face on it; and as he needed somebody to carry a message into the enemy's camp, he bethought himself of a plan which succeeded perfectly.

For several days he had watched little Mariette, and assured himself that she took a daily walk in the direction of Dollins, where Sévère lived, and that she was on more friendly terms with this woman than he could wish, chiefly because she met at her house all her young acquaintances, and some men from town who made love to her. She did not listen to them, for she was still an innocent girl, and had no idea that the wolf was so near the sheepfold, but she loved flattery, and was as thirsty for it as a fly for milk. She kept her walks secret from Madeleine; and as Madeleine never gossiped with the other women, and had not as yet left her sickroom, she guessed nothing, and suspected no evil. Big Catherine was the last person in the world to notice anything, so that the little girl cocked her cap over her ear, and, under the pretext of driving the sheep to pasture, she soon left them in charge of some little shepherd-boy, and was off to play the fine lady in poor company.

François, however, who was going continually to and fro on the affairs of the mill, took note of what the girl was doing. He never mentioned it at home, but turned it to account, as you shall hear.

CHAPTER XXI

H E PLANTED HIMSELF directly in her way at the river-crossing; and just as she stepped on the footbridge which leads to Dollins, she beheld the waif, astride of the plank, a leg dangling on each side above the water, and on his face the expression of a man who has all the time in the world to spare. She blushed as red as a cherry, and if she had not been taken so by surprise, she would have swerved aside, and pretended to be passing by accident.

But the approach to the bridge was obstructed by branches, and she did not see the wolf till she felt his teeth. His face was turned towards her, so she had no means of advancing or retreating, without being observed.

'Master Miller,' she began, saucily, 'can't you move a hairbreadth to let anybody pass?'

'No, my young lady,' replied François, 'for I am the guardian of this bridge till evening, and I claim the right to collect toll of everybody.'

'Are you mad, François? Nobody pays toll in our country, and you have no right on any bridge, or footbridge, or whatever you may call it in your country of Aigurande. You may say what you like, but take yourself off from here, as quickly as you can; this is not the place for jesting; you will make me tumble into the water.'

'Then,' said François, without moving, and folding his arms in front of him, 'you think that I want to laugh and joke with you, and that my right of toll is that of paying you my court? Pray get rid of that idea, my young lady; I wish to speak sensibly to you, and I will allow you to pass if you give me permission to accompany you for a short part of your way.'

'That would not be at all proper,' said Mariette, somewhat flustered by her notion of what François was thinking. 'What would they say of me hereabouts, if anybody met me out walking alone with a man to whom I am not betrothed?'

'You are right,' said François; 'as Sévère is not here to protect you, people would talk of you; that is why you are going to her house, so that you may walk about in her garden with all your admirers. Very well, so as not to embarrass you, I shall speak to you here, and briefly, for my business is pressing, and this it is. You are a good girl; you love your sister-in-law Madeleine; you see that she is in difficulties, and you must want to help her out of them.'

'If that is what you want to say,' returned Mariette, 'I shall listen to you, for you are speaking the truth.'

'Very well, my dear young lady,' said François, rising and leaning beside her, against the bank beside the little bridge, 'you can do a great service to Madame Blanchet. Since it is for her good and interest, as I fondly believe, that you are so friendly with Sévère, you must make that woman agree to a compromise. Sévère is trying to attain two objects which are incompatible: she wants to make Master Blanchet's estate security for the payment of the land he sold for the purpose of paying his debts to her; and in the second place, she means to exact payment of the notes which he signed in her favour. She may go to law, if she likes, and wrangle about this poor little estate, but she cannot succeed in getting more out of it than there is. Make her understand that if she does not insist upon our guaranteeing the payment of the land, we can pay her notes; but if she does not allow us to get rid of one debt, we shall not have funds enough to pay the other, and if she makes us drain ourselves with expenses which bring her no profit, she runs the risk of losing everything.'

'That is true,' said Mariette; 'although I understand very little about business, I think I can understand as much as that. If I am able, by any chance, to influence her, which would be better: for my sister-in-law to pay the notes, or to be obliged to redeem the security?'

'It would be worse for her to pay the notes, for it would be more unjust. We could contest the notes and go to law about them; but the law requires money, and you know that there is none, and never will be any, at the mill. So, it is all one to your sister, whether her little all goes in a lawsuit or in paying Sévère; whereas it is better for Sévère to be paid, without having a lawsuit.

'As Madeleine is sure to be ruined in either case, she prefers to have all her possessions seized at once than to drag on after this under a heavy burden of debt, which may last all her lifetime; for the purchasers of Cadet Blanchet's land are not able to pay for it. Sévère knows this well, and will be forced, some fine day, to take back her land; but this idea is not at all distressing to her, as it will be a profitable speculation for her to receive the land in an improved condition, having long drawn a heavy rate of interest from it. Thus, Sévère risks nothing in setting us free, and assures the payment of her notes.'

'I shall do as you say,' said Mariette; 'and if I fail, you may think as ill of me as you choose.'

'Then good luck, Mariette, and a pleasant walk to you,' said François, stepping out of her way.

Little Mariette started off to Dollins, well pleased to have such a fine excuse for going there, for staying a long time, and for returning often during the next few days. Sévère pretended to like what she heard, but she really determined to be in no haste. She had always hated Madeleine Blanchet, because of the involuntary respect her husband had felt for her. She thought she held her safely in her claws for the whole of her lifetime, and preferred to give up the notes, which she knew to be of no great value, rather than renounce the pleasure of harassing her with the burden of an endless debt.

François understood all this perfectly, and was anxious to induce her to exact the payment of this debt, so that he might have an opportunity to buy back Jennie's broad fields from those who had purchased them for a song. When Mariette returned with her answer, he saw that they were trying to mislead him with words; that, on one hand, the young girl was glad to have her errands last for a long time to come, and that, on the other hand. Sévère had not reached the point of being more desirous for Madeleine's rain than for the payment of her notes.

To clinch matters, he took Mariette aside, two days afterwards.

'My dear young lady,' said he, 'you must not go to Dollins today. Your sister has learned, though I do not know how, that you go there more than once a day, and she says it is no place for a respectable girl. I have tried to make her understand that it is for her interest that you are so friendly with Sévère; but she blamed me as well as you. She says that she would rather be ruined than have you lose your reputation, that you are under her guardianship, and that she has authority over you. If you do not obey of your own free will, you will be prevented from going by main force. If you do as she says, she will not mention this to you, as she wishes to avoid giving you pain, but she is very much displeased with you, and it would be well for you to beg her pardon.'

François had no sooner unleashed the dog than it began to bark and bite. He was correct in his estimate of little Mariette's temper, which was as hasty and inflammable as her brother's had been.

'Indeed, indeed!' she exclaimed; 'do you expect me to obey my sister-in-law, as if I were a child of three? You talk as if she were my mother, and I owed her submission! What makes her think that I may lose my reputation? Tell her that it is quite as well buckled on as her own, and perhaps better. Why does she imagine that Sévère is not so good as other people? Is it wicked not to spend the whole day sewing, spinning and praying? My sister-in-law is unjust because she has a quarrel with her about money, and she thinks she can treat her as she pleases. It is very imprudent of her, for if Sévère wished she could turn her out of the house she lives in; and as Sévère is patient, and does not make use of her advantage, she is certainly better than she is said to be. And this is the way in which you thank me, who have been obliging enough to take part in these disputes, which are no concern of mine! I can tell you, François, that the most respectable people are not always the most prudish, and when I go to Sévère's I do no more mischief than if I stayed at home.'

'I don't know about that,' said François, who was determined to make all the scum of the vat mount to the surface; 'perhaps your sister was right in thinking that you are in some mischief there. Look here, Mariette, I see that you like to go there too well. It is not natural. You have delivered your message about Madeleine's affairs, and since Sévère has sent no answer, it is evident that she means to give none. Do not go back there any more, or I shall think, with Madeleine, that you go with no good intention.'

'Then, Master François,' cried Mariette, in a fury, 'you think you are going to dictate to me? Do you mean to take my brother's place at home, and make yourself master there? You have not enough beard on your chin to give me such a lecture, and I advise you to leave me alone. Your humble servant,' she added, adjusting her coif; 'if my sister-in-law asks where I am, tell her that I am at Sévère's, and if she sends you after me, you will see how you are received.'

She burst the door open violently, and flew off with a light foot towards Dollins; but as François was afraid that her anger would cool on the way, especially as the weather was frosty, he allowed her a little start. He waited until he thought she had nearly reached Sévère's house, and then, putting his long legs in motion, he ran like a horse let loose, and caught up with her, to make her believe that Madeleine had sent him in pursuit of her.

He was so provoking that she raised her hand against him. He dodged her every time, being well aware that anger evaporates with blows, and that a woman's temper improves when she has relieved herself by striking. Then he ran away, and as soon as Mariette arrived at Sévère's house she made a great explosion. The poor child had really no bad designs; but in the first flame of her anger she disclosed everything, and put Sévère into such a towering passion that François, who was retreating noiselessly through the lane, heard them at the other end of the hemp-field, hissing and crackling like fire in a barn full of hay.

CHAPTER XXII

H IS PLAN SUCCEEDED admirably, and he was so sure of it that he went over to Aigurande next day, took his money from the priest and returned at night, carrying the four little notes of thin paper, which were of such great value, and yet made no more noise in his pocket than a crumb of bread in a cap. After a week's time, Sévère made herself heard. All the purchasers of Blanchet's land were summoned to pay up, and as not one was able to do it, Sévère threatened to make Madeleine pay instead.

Madeleine was much alarmed when she heard the news, for she had received no hint from François of what was coming.

'Good!' said he to her, rubbing his hands. 'A trader cannot always gain, nor a thief always rob. Madame Sévère is going to make a bad bargain and you a good one. All the same, my dear mother, you must behave as if you thought you were ruined. The sadder you are, the gladder she will be to do what she thinks is to your harm. But that harm is your salvation, for when you pay Sévère you will buy back your son's inheritance.'

'What do you expect me to pay her with, my child?'

'With the money I have in my pocket, and which belongs to you.'

Madeleine tried to dissuade him; but the waif was headstrong, as he said himself, and no one could loose what he had bound. He hastened to deposit two hundred pistoles with the notary, in the widow Blanchet's name, and Sévère was paid in full, willingly or unwillingly, and also all the other creditors of the estate, who had made common cause with her.

Moreover, after François had indemnified all the poor purchasers of the land for their losses, he had still enough money with which to go to law, and he let Sévère know that he was about to embark in a lawsuit on the subject of the promissory notes which she had wrongfully and fraudulently extracted from the miller. He set afloat a report which spread far and wide through the land. He pretended that in fumbling about an old wall of the mill which he was trying to prop up, he had found old Mother Blanchet's money box, filled with gold coins of an ancient stamp, and that by this means Madeleine was richer than she had ever been. Weary of warfare, Sévère consented to a compromise, hoping also that François would be lavish of the crowns which he had so opportunely discovered, and that she could wheedle from him more than he gave her to expect. She got nothing for her pains, however, and he was so hard with her that she was forced to return the notes in exchange for a hundred crowns.

To revenge herself, she worked upon little Mariette, telling her that the money box of old Mother Blanchet, who was the girl's grandmother, should have been divided between her and Jeannie, that she had a right to her share, and should go to law against her sister.

Then the waif was forced to tell the true source of the money he had provided, and the priest of Aigurande sent him the proofs, in case of there being a lawsuit.

He began by showing these proofs to Mariette, begging her to make no unnecessary disclosures, and making it dear to her that she had better keep quiet. But Mariette would not keep at all quiet; her little brain was excited by the confusion in the family, and the devil tempted the poor child. In spite of all the kindness she had received from Madeleine, who had treated her as a daughter and indulged all her whims, she felt a dislike and jealousy of her sister-in-law, although her pride prevented her from acknowledging it. The truth is that in the midst of her tantrums and quarrels with François, she had inadvertently fallen in love with him, and never suspected the trap which the devil had set for her. The more François upbraided her for her faults and vagaries, the more crazy she was to please him.

She was not the kind of girl to pine and consume away in grief and tears; but it robbed her of her peace to think that François was so handsome, rich and upright, so kind to everybody, and so clever and brave; that he was a man to shed his last drop of blood for the woman he loved, and yet that none of this was for her, although she was the prettiest and richest girl in the neighbourhood, and counted her lovers by the dozen.

One day she opened her heart to her false friend, Sévère. It was in the pasture at the end of the road of the water lilies, underneath an old apple tree that was then in blossom. While all these things were happening, the month of May had come, and Sévère strolled out under the apple blossoms, to chat with Mariette, who was tending her flock beside the river.

It pleased God that François, who was nearby, should overhear their conversation. He had seen Sévère enter the pasture, and at once suspected her of meditating some intrigue against Madeleine; and as the river was low, he walked noiselessly along the bank, beneath the bushes which are so tall just there that a hay-cart could pass under their shade. When he came within hearing distance, he sat down on the ground, without making a sound, and opened his ears very wide.

The two women plied their tongues busily. In the first place, Mariette confessed to not caring for a single one of her suitors, for the sake of a young miller, who was not at all courteous to her, and the thought of whom kept her awake at night. Sévère, on the other hand, wanted to unite her to a young man of her acquaintance, who was so much in love with the girl that he had promised a handsome wedding present to Sévère if she succeeded in marrying him to Mariette Blanchet. It appeared also that Sévère had exacted a gratuity beforehand from him and from several others; so she naturally did all in her power to put Mariette out of conceit with François.

'A plague take the waif!' she exclaimed. 'What, Mariette, a girl in your position marry a foundling! You would be called Madame Strawberry, for he has no other name. I should be ashamed for you, my poor darling. Then you have no chance; you would be obliged to light for him with your sister-in-law, for he is her lover, as true as I live.'

'Sévère,' cried Mariette, 'you have hinted this to me more than once; but I cannot believe you; my sister-in-law is too old.'

'No, no, Mariette; your sister-in-law is not old enough to do without this sort of thing; she is only thirty, and when the waif was but a boy, your brother discovered that he was too familiar with his wife. That is why he gave him a sound thrashing with the butt of his whip, and turned him out of doors.'

François felt a lively desire to spring out of the bushes and tell Sévère that she lied; but he restrained himself, and sat motionless.

Sévère continued to ring the changes on this subject, and told so many shocking lies that François's face burned, and it was with great difficulty that he kept his patience.

'Then,' said Mariette, 'he probably means to marry her now that she is a widow; he has already given her a good part of his fortune, and he must wish to have a share in the property which he has bought back.'

'Somebody else will outbid him,' said the other; 'for now that Madeleine has plundered him, she will be on the lookout for a richer suitor, and will be sure to find one. She must take a husband to manage her property, but while she is trying to find him, she keeps this great simpleton with her, who serves her for nothing, and amuses her solitude.'

'If she is going along at that pace,' said Mariette, much vexed, 'I am in a most disreputable house; in which I run too many dangers! Do you consider, my dear Sévère, that I am very ill-lodged, and that people will talk against me? Indeed, I cannot stay where I am; I must leave. Oh! Yes, these pious women criticise everybody else, because they themselves are shameless only in God's sight! I should like to hear her say anything against you and me now! Very well! I am going to say goodbye to her, and I am coming to live with you; if she is angry, I shall answer her; if she tries to bring me back by force to live with her, I shall go to law; and I shall let people know what she is – do you hear?'

'A better remedy for you, Mariette, is to get married as soon as possible. She will not refuse her consent, because I am sure she is anxious to rid herself of you. You stand in the way of her relations with the handsome waif. You must not delay, cannot you understand, for people will say that he belongs to both of you, and then nobody will marry you. Go and get married, then, and take the man I advise.'

'Agreed,' said Mariette, breaking her shepherd's crook violently, against the old apple tree. 'I give you my word. Go and tell him, Sévère; let him come to my house this evening, to ask for my hand, and let our banns be published next Sunday.'

CHAPTER XXIII

FRANÇOIS WAS NEVER sadder than when he emerged from the riverbank where he had hidden himself to listen to the women's talk. His heart was as heavy as lead, and when he had gone halfway home he lost courage to return, and, stepping aside into the path of the water-lilies, he sat down in the little grove of oaks at the end of the meadow.

Once there, by himself, he wept like a child, and his heart was bursting with sorrow and shame; for he was ashamed to hear of what he was accused, and to think that his poor dear friend Madeleine, whom, through all his life, he had loved so purely and constantly, reaped nothing but insult and slander from his devotion and fidelity.

'Oh! My God, my God!' said he to himself. 'How can it be that the world is so wicked and that a woman like Sévère can have the insolence to measure the honour of a woman like my dear mother, by her own standard? And that little Mariette, who should naturally be inclined to innocence and truth, a child as she is, who does not as yet know the meaning of evil, even she listens to this infernal calumny, and believes in it, as if she knew how it stung! Since this is so, others will believe it too; as the larger part of people living mortal life are old in evil, almost everybody win think that because I love Madame Blanchet, and she loves me, there must be something dishonourable in it.'

Then poor François undertook a careful examination of his conscience, and searched his memory to see whether, by any fault of his, he were responsible for Sévère's wicked gossip; whether he had behaved wisely in all respects, or whether, by a lack of prudence and discretion, he had involuntarily given rise to evil thinking. But it was in vain that he reflected, for he could not believe that he had appeared guilty of what had never even crossed his mind.

Still absorbed in thought and reverie, he went on saying to himself: 'Suppose that my liking had turned to loving, what harm would it be in God's sight, now that she is a widow and her own mistress? I have given a good part of my fortune to her and Jeannie, but I still have a considerable share left, and she would not wrong her child if she married me. It would not be self-seeking on my part to desire this, and nobody could make her believe that my love for her is self-interested. I am a foundling, but she does not care for that. She has loved me with a mother's love, which is the strongest of all affections, and now she might love me in another way. I see that her enemies will force me to leave her if I do not marry her, and I should rather die than leave her a second time. Besides, she needs my help, and I should be a coward to leave her affairs in such disorder when I have strength as well as money with which to serve her. Yes, all I have should belong to her, and as she often talks to me about paying me back in the end, I must put that idea out of her head, by sharing all things in common with her, in accordance with the permission of God and the law. She must keep her good name for her son's sake, and she can save it only by marrying me. How is it that I never thought of this before, and that I needed to hear it suggested by a serpent's tongue? I was too simple-minded and unsuspecting; and my poor mother is too charitable to others to take to heart the injuries which are done her. Everything tends towards good, by the will of Heaven; and Madame Sévère, who was plotting mischief, has done me the service of teaching me my duty.'

Without indulging any longer in meditation or wonder, François set off on his way home, determined to speak of his plan to Madame Blanchet without loss of time, and on his knees to entreat her to accept him as her protector, in the name of God, and for eternal life.

When he reached Cormouer, he saw Madeleine spinning on her doorstep, and for the first time in his life her face had the effect of making him timid and confused. He was in the habit of walking straight up to her, looking her full in the face to ask her how she did; but this time he paused on the little bridge as if he were examining the mill-dam, and only looked at her out of the corners of his eyes.

When she turned towards him, he moved further away, not understanding himself what his trouble was, or why a matter which, a few minutes ago, had seemed to him so natural and opportune, should suddenly become so awkward to confess.

Madeleine called him.

'Come here to me,' said she, 'for I have something to say to you, dear François. We are alone, so come and sit down beside me, and open your heart to me, as if I were your father confessor, for I want to hear the truth from you.'

François was reassured by Madeleine's words, and he sat down beside her.

'I promise, my dear mother,' said he, 'to open my heart to you as I do to God, and to give you a true confession.'

He fancied that something had come to her ears which had brought her to the same conclusion as himself; he was delighted, and waited to hear what she had to say.

'François,' she went on, 'you are in your twenty-first year, and it is time for you to think of marrying; you are not opposed to it, I hope?'

'No, I am not opposed to anything you wish,' answered François, blushing with pleasure; 'go on, my dear Madeleine.'

'Good!' said she. 'I expected this, and I have guessed the right thing. Since you wish it, I wish it too, and perhaps I thought of it before you did. I was waiting to see whether the person in question cared for you, and I think that if she does not as yet, she will, very soon. Don't you think so, too, and shall I tell you where you stand? Why do you look at me with such a puzzled expression? Don't I speak clearly enough? I see that you are shy about it, and I must help you out. Well, the poor child pouted all the morning because you teased her a little yesterday, and I dare say she thinks you do not love her. But I know that you do love her, and if you scold her sometimes for her little caprices it is because you are a trifle jealous. You must not hold back for that, François. She is young and pretty; but though there is some danger in this, if she truly loves you she will willingly submit herself to you.'

'I should like,' said François, much disappointed, 'to know whom you are talking of, my dear mother, for I am wholly at a loss.'

'Really!' said Madeleine. 'Don't you know what I mean? Am I dreaming, or are you trying to keep a secret from me?'

'A secret from you!' said François, taking Madeleine's hand. He soon dropped it, and took up instead the corner of her apron, which he crumpled as if he were provoked, then lifted towards his lips as if about to kiss it, and finally let go just as he had done with her hand. He was first inclined to cry; then he felt angry, and then giddy, all in succession.

Madeleine was amazed.

'You are in trouble, my child,' she cried, 'and this means that you are in love – that all does not go as you wish. I can assure you that Mariette has a good heart; she, too, is distressed, and if you speak openly with her she will tell you, in return, that she thinks of no one but you.'

François sprang up, and walked up and down the courtyard for some time in silence; then he returned to Madeleine's side.

'I am very much surprised to hear what you have in your mind, Madame Blanchet; this never once occurred to me, and I am well aware that Mariette has no liking for me, and that I am not to her taste.'

'Oh, come!' said Madeleine. 'You are speaking petulantly, my child! Don't you think I noticed how often you talked with her? Though I could not catch the meaning of what you said, it was evident that she understood very well, for her face glowed like a burning coal. Do you think I do not know that she runs away from the pasture every day, leaving her flock in charge of the first person she meets? Her sheep flourish at the expense of our wheat; but I do not want to cross her, or talk to her of sheep, when her head is full of nothing but love and marriage. The poor child is just of an age to guard her sheep ill, and her heart still worse. But it is great good luck for her, François, that instead of falling in love with one of those bad fellows whom I was so much afraid of her meeting at Sévère's, she had the good sense to think of you. It makes me, too, very happy to think that, when you are married to my sister-in-law, who is almost the same as a daughter to me, you will live with me and make part of my family, and that I may harbour you in my house, work with you, bring up your children, and thus repay your kindness to me. So do not let your childish notions interfere with all the joys I have planned. Try to see clearly, and forget your jealousy. If Mariette is fond of dress, it is because she is anxious to please you. If she has been rather idle lately, it is only because she is thinking too much of you; and if she answers me sometimes rather sharply, she does so because she is vexed with your reprimands, and does not know whom to blame for them. The proof that she is good and desirous of mending her ways, is that she has recognised your goodness and wisdom, and wants you for her husband.'

'You are good, my dear mother,' said François, quite crestfallen. 'Yes, it is you who are good, for you believe in the goodness of others and deceive yourself. I can tell you that, if Mariette is good, too, and I will not say she is not, lest I should injure her in your opinion, it is in a way very different from yours, and, consequently, very displeasing to me. Do not say anything more to me about her. I swear to you on my word and honour, on my heart and soul, that I am no more in love with her than I am with old Catherine, and if she has any regard for me, it is her own misfortune, because I cannot return it. Do not try to make her say she loves me; your tact would be at fault, and you would make her my enemy. It is quite the contrary; hear what she will say to you tonight, and let her marry Jean Aubard, whom she has made up her mind to accept. Let her marry as soon as possible, for she is out of place in your house. She is not happy there, and will not be a source of comfort to you.'

'Jean Aubard!' exclaimed Madeleine. 'He is not a proper person for her; he is a fool, and she is too clever to submit herself to a stupid man.'

'He is rich, and she will not submit to him. She will manage him, and he is just the man for her. Will you not trust in your friend, my dear mother? You know that, up to this time, I have never given you any bad advice. Let the young girl go; she does not love you as she ought, and she does not know your worth.'

'You say this because your feelings are hurt, François,' said Madeleine, laying her hand on his head and moving it gently up and down, as if she were trying to shake the truth out of it François was exasperated that she would not believe him, and it was the first time in his life that there had been any dispute between them. He withdrew, saying in a dissatisfied tone of voice:

'Madame Blanchet, you are not just to me. I tell you that girl does not love you. You force me to say this, against my will; for I did not come here to bring distrust and strife. So, if I tell it to you, you may know that I am sure of it; and do you think I can love her after that? You cannot love me any more, if you will not believe me.'

Wild with grief, François rushed off to weep all alone by the fountain.

CHAPTER XXIV

MADELEINE WAS still more perplexed than François, and was on the point of following him with questions and words of encouragement; but she was held back by the sudden appearance of Mariette, who, with a strange expression on her face, announced the offer of marriage she had received from Jean Aubard. Madeleine, who was unable to disabuse herself of the idea that the whole affair was the result of a lovers' quarrel, attempted to speak to the girl of François; but Mariette answered in a tone which gave her great pain, and was utterly incomprehensible to her:

'Those people who care for foundlings may keep them for their own amusement; I am an honest girl, and shall not allow my good name to suffer because my poor brother is dead. I am perfectly independent, Madeleine; and if I am forced by law to ask your advice, I am not forced to take it when it is not for my good. So please do not stand in my way, or I may stand in yours hereafter.'

'I cannot imagine what is the matter with you, my dear child,' said Madeleine, very sweetly and sadly. 'You speak to me as if you had neither respect nor affection for me.

I think you must be in some distress which has confused your mind; so I entreat you to take three or four days, in which to decide. I shall tell Jean Aubard to come back, and if you are of the same opinion after a little quiet reflection, I shall give you free leave to marry him, as he is a respectable man, and comfortably off. But you are in such an excited condition, just now, that you cannot know your own mind, and you shut your heart against my affection. You grieve me very much, but as I see that you are grieved too, I forgive you.'

Mariette tossed her head, to show how much she despised that sort of forgiveness, and ran away to put on her silk apron and prepare for the reception of Jean Aubard, who arrived, an hour later, with big Sévère in gala dress.

This time, at last, Madeleine was convinced of Mariette's ill will towards her, since the girl had brought into her house, on a family matter, a woman who was her enemy, and whom she blushed to see. Notwithstanding this, she advanced very politely to meet Sévère, and served her with refreshments, without any appearance of anger or dislike; for she feared that if Mariette were opposed, she would prove unmanageable. So Madeleine said that she made no objection to her sister-in-law's desire, but requested three days' grace before giving her answer.

Thereupon Sévère said, insolently, that was a very long time to wait. Madeleine answered quietly that it was a very short time.

Jean Aubard then left, looking like a blockhead, and giggling like a booby, for he was sure that Mariette was madly in love with him. He had paid well for this illusion, and Sévère gave him his money's worth.

As Sévère left the house, she said to Mariette that she had ordered a cake and some sweets at home for the betrothal, and even if Madame Blanchet delayed the preliminaries, they must sit down to the feast. Madeleine objected that it was not proper for a young girl to go off in the company of a man who had not as yet received his answer from her family.

'If that is so, I shall not go,' said Mariette, in a huff.

'Oh, yes, yes; you must come,' Sévère insisted. 'Are not you your own mistress?'

'No, indeed,' returned Mariette; 'you see my sister-in-law forbids me to go.'

She went into her room and slammed the door; but she merely passed through the house, went out by the back door, and caught up with Sévère and her suitor at the end of the meadow, laughing and jeering at Madeleine's expense.

Poor Madeleine could not restrain her tears when she saw how things were going.

'François was right,' thought she; 'the girl does not love me, and she is ungrateful at heart. She will not believe that I am acting for her good, that I am most anxious for her happiness, and wish only to prevent her doing something which she will regret hereafter. She has taken evil counsel, and I am condemned to see that wretched Sévère stirring up trouble and strife in my family. I have not deserved all these troubles, and I must submit to God's will. Fortunately, poor François was more clear-sighted than I. How much he would suffer with such a wife!'

She went to look for him, to let him know what she thought; but when she found him in tears beside the fountain, she supposed he was grieving for the loss of Mariette, and attempted to comfort him. The more she said the more pained he was, for it became clear to him that she refused to understand the truth, and that her heart could never feel for him in the way he had hoped.

In the evening, when Jeannie was in bed and asleep, François sat with Madeleine, and sought to explain himself.

He began by saying that Mariette was jealous of her, and that Sévère had slandered her infamously; but Madeleine never dreamed of his meaning.

'What can she say against me?' said she, simply. 'And what jealousy can she put into poor silly little Mariette's head? You are mistaken, François; something else is at stake, some interested reason which we shall hear later. It is not possible that she should be jealous; I am too old to give any anxiety to a young and pretty girl. I am almost thirty, and for a peasant woman who has undergone a great deal of trouble and fatigue, that is old enough to be your mother. The devil only could say that I think of you in any way but as my son, and Mariette must know I longed to have you both marry. No, no; never believe that she has any such evil thought, or, at least, do not mention it to me, for I should be too much pained and mortified.'

'And yet,' said François, making a great effort to speak, and bending low over the fire to hide his confusion from Madeleine, 'Monsieur Blanchet had some such evil thought when he turned me out of doors!'

'What! Do you know that now, François?' exclaimed Madeleine. 'How is it that you know it? I never told you, and I never should have told you. If Catherine spoke of it to you, she did wrong. Such an idea must shock and pain you as much as it does me, but we must try not to think of it any more, and to forgive my husband, now that he is dead.

All the obloquy of it falls upon Sévère; but now Sévère can be no longer jealous of me. I have no husband, and I am as old and ugly as she could ever have wished, though I am not in the least sorry for it, for I have gained the right of being respected, of treating you as a son, and of finding you a pretty young wife, who will live happily with me and love me as a mother. This is my only wish, François, and you must not distress yourself, for we shall find her. So much the worse for Mariette if she despises the happiness I had in store for her. Now, go to bed, my child, and take courage. If I thought I were any obstacle to your marrying, I should send you away at once; but you may be sure that nobody worries about me, or imagines what is absolutely impossible.'

As François listened to Madeleine, he was convinced that she was right, so accustomed was he to believe all that she said. He rose to bid her goodnight, but, as he took her hand, it happened that, for the first time in his life, he looked at her with the intention of finding out whether she were old and ugly; and the truth is, she had long been so sad and serious that she deceived herself, and was still as pretty a woman as she had ever been.

So when François saw all at once that she was still young and as beautiful as the blessed Virgin, his heart gave a great bound, as if he had climbed to the pinnacle of a tower. He went back for the night to the mill, where his bed was neatly spread in a square of boards among the sacks of flour. Once there, and by himself, he shivered and gasped as if he had a fever; but it was only the fever of love, for he who had all his life warmed himself comfortably in front of the ashes, had suddenly been scorched by a great burst of flame.

CHAPTER XXV

FROM THAT TIME ON, the waif was so melancholy that it made one's heart ache to see him. He worked like a horse, but he found no more joy or peace, and Madeleine could not induce him to say what was the matter with him. It was in vain he swore that he neither loved nor regretted Mariette, for Madeleine would not believe him, and could assign no other cause for his depression. She was grieved that he should be in distress and yet no longer confide in her, and she was amazed that his trouble should make him so proud and self-willed.

As it was not in her nature to be tormenting, she made up her mind to say nothing further to him on the subject. She attempted to make Mariette reverse her decision, but her overtures were so ill-received that she lost courage, and was silent. Though her heart was full of anguish, she kept it to herself, lest she should add to the burden of others.

François worked for her, and served her with the same zeal and devotion as before. As in the old time, he stayed as much as possible in her company, but he no longer spoke as he used. He was always embarrassed with her, and turned first red as fire, and then white as a sheet in the same minute. She was afraid he was ill, and once took his hand to see if he were feverish; but he drew back from her as if her touch hurt him, and sometimes he reproached her in words which she could not understand.

The trouble between them grew from day to day. During all this time, great preparations were being made for Mariette's marriage to Jean Aubard, and the day which was to end her mourning was fixed as that of the wedding.

Madeleine looked forward to that day with dread; she feared that François would go crazy, and was anxious to send him to spend a little time at Aigurande, with his old master Jean Vertaud, so as to distract his mind. François, however, was unwilling to let Mariette believe what Madeleine insisted upon thinking. He showed no vexation before her, was on friendly relations with her lover, and jested with Sévère, when he met her along the road, to let her see that he had nothing to fear from her. He was present at the wedding; and as he was really delighted to have the house rid of the girl, and Madeleine freed from her false friendship, it never crossed anybody's mind that he had been in love with her. The truth began to dawn even on Madeleine, or at least she was inclined to believe that he had consoled himself. She received Mariette's farewell with her accustomed warmth of heart; but as the young girl still cherished a grudge against her on account of the waif, Madeleine could not help seeing that her sister-in-law left her without love or regret. Inured as she was to sorrow, Madeleine wept over the girl's hardness of heart, and prayed God to forgive her.

After a week had passed, François unexpectedly told her that he had some business at Aigurande that would call him there for the space of five or six days. She was not surprised, and hoped it would be for the good of his health, for she believed that he had stifled his grief, and was ill in consequence.

But that grief, which she thought he had overcome, increased with him day by day. He could think of nothing else, and whether asleep or awake, far or near, Madeleine was always in his heart and before his eyes. It is true that all his life had been spent in loving her and thinking of her, but until lately these thoughts of her had been has happiness and consolation, whereas they were now his despair and his undoing. As long as he was content to be her son and friend, he wished for no better lot on earth; but now his love had changed its character, and he was exquisitely unhappy. He fancied that she could never change as he had done. He kept repeating to himself that he was too young, that she had known him as a forlorn and wretched child, that he could be only an object of care and compassion to her, and never of pride. In short, he believed her to be so lovely and so attractive, so far above him, and so much to be desired, that when she said she was no longer young and pretty, he thought she was adopting a role to scare away her suitors.

In the mean time, Sévère, Mariette, and their clan were slandering her openly on his account, and he was in terror lest some of the scandal should come to her ears, and she should be displeased and long for his departure. He knew she was too kind to ask him to go, but he dreaded being again a cause of annoyance to her, as he had been once before, and it occurred to him to go to ask the advice of the priest of Aigurande, whom he had found to be a just and God-fearing man.

He went, but with no success, as the priest was absent on a visit to his bishop; so François returned to the mill of Jean

Vertaud, who had invited him for a few days' visit, while waiting for the priest's return.

He found his kind master as true a man and as faithful a friend as he had left him, and his good daughter Jeannette on the brink of marriage with a very respectable man whom she had accepted from motives of prudence rather than of enthusiasm, but for whom she fortunately felt more liking than distaste. This put François more at his ease with her than he had ever been, and the next day being Sunday, he had a long talk with her, and confided in her Madame Blanchet's many difficulties, and his satisfaction in rescuing her from them.

Jeannette was quick-witted, and from one thing and another she guessed that the waif was more agitated by his attachment to Madeleine than he would confess. She laid her hand on his arm, and said to him abruptly:

'François, you must hide nothing from me. I have come to my senses now, and you see that I am not ashamed to tell you that I once thought more of you than you did of me. You knew my feelings, and you could not return them, but you would not deceive me, and no selfish interest led you to do what many others would have done in your place. I respect you both for your behaviour towards me and for your constancy to the woman you loved best in the world; and instead of disowning my regard for you, I am glad to remember it. I expect you to think the better of me for acknowledging it, and to do me the justice to observe that I bear no grudge or malice towards you for your coolness. I mean to give you the greatest possible token of my esteem. You love Madeleine Blanchet, not indeed as a mother, but as a young and attractive woman, whom you wish for your wife.'

'Oh!' said François, blushing like a girl. 'I love her as a mother, and my heart is full of respect for her.'

'I have no doubt of it,' answered Jeannette; 'but you love her in two ways, for your face says one thing and your words another. Very well, François; you dare not tell her what you dare not even confess to me, and you do not know whether she can answer your two ways of loving.'

Jeannette Vertaud spoke with so much sense and sweetness, and showed François such true friendship, that he had not the courage to deceive her, and, pressing her hand, he told her that she was like a sister to him, and the only person in the world to whom he had the heart to disclose his secret.

Jeannette asked him several questions, which he answered truly and openly.

'François, my friend,' said she, 'I understand it all. It is impossible for me to know what Madeleine Blanchet will think about it; but I see that you might be for years in her company without having the boldness to tell her what you have on your mind. No matter. I shall find out for you, and shall let you know. My father and you and I shall set out tomorrow for a friendly visit to Cormouer, as if we went to make the acquaintance of the kind woman who brought up our friend François; you must take my father to walk about the place, under pretext of asking his advice, and I shall spend the time talking with Madeleine. I shall use a great deal of tact, and shall not tell what your feelings are until I am certain of hers.'

François was so grateful to Jeannette that he was ready to fall on his knees before her; and Jean Vertaud, who, with the waif's permission, was informed of the situation, gave his consent to the plan. Next day they set out; Jeannette rode on the croup behind her father, and François started an hour earlier than they to prepare Madeleine for the visit she was to receive.

The sun was setting as François approached Cormouer. A storm came up during his ride, and he was drenched to the skin; but he never murmured, for he had good hope in Jeannette's friendly offices, and his heart was lighter than when he had left home. The water was dripping from the bushes, and the blackbirds were singing like mad in thankfulness for a last gleam from the sun before it sank behind the hill of Grand-Corlay. Great flocks of birds fluttered from branch to branch around François, and their joyous chattering cheered his spirits. He thought of the time when he was little, and roamed about the meadows, whistling to attract the birds, absorbed in his childish dreams and fancies. Just then a handsome bullfinch hovered round his head, like a harbinger of good luck and good tidings, and his thoughts wandered back to his Mother Zabelle and the quaint songs of the olden time, with which she used to sing him to sleep.

Madeleine did not expect him so soon. She had even feared that he would never come back at all, and when she caught sight of him she could not help running to kiss him, and was surprised to see how much it made him blush. He announced the approaching visit, and apparently as much afraid of having her guess his feelings as he was grieved to have her ignore them, in order to prevent her suspecting anything, he told her that Jean Vertaud thought of buying some land in the neighbourhood.

Then Madeleine bestirred herself to prepare the best entertainment she could offer to François's friends.

Jeannette was the first to enter the house, while her father was putting up their horse in the stable; and as soon as she saw Madeleine she took a great liking for her, a liking which the other woman fully returned. They began by shaking hands, but they soon fell to kissing each other for the sake of their common love for François, and they spoke together freely, as if they had had a long and intimate acquaintance. The truth is they were both excellent women, and made such a pair as is hard to find. Jeannette could not help a pang on seeing Madeleine, whom she knew to be idolised by the man for whom she herself still cherished a lingering fondness; but she felt no jealousy, and tried to forget her grief in the good action on which she was bent. On the other hand, when Madeleine saw the young woman's sweet face and graceful figure, she supposed that it was she whom François had loved and pined for, that they were now betrothed, and that Jeannette had come to bring the news in person; but neither did she feel any jealousy, for she had never thought of François save as her own child.

In the evening, after supper, Father Vertaud, who was tired by his ride, went to bed; and Jeannette took Madeleine out into the garden with her, after first instructing François to keep a little aloof with Jeannie, but still near enough to see her let down the corner of her apron, which she wore tucked up on one side, for this was to be the signal for him to join them. She then fulfilled her mission conscientiously, and so skilfully that Madeleine had no time to exclaim, although beyond measure astonished, as the matter was unfolded to her. At first she thought it but another proof of François's goodness of heart, that he wished to put a stop to all evil gossip, and to devote his life to her service; and she would have refused, thinking it too great a sacrifice on the part of so young a man to marry a woman older than himself. She feared he would repent later, and could not long keep his faith to her, without vexation and regret; but Jeannette gave her to understand that the waif was in love with her, heart and soul, and that he was losing his health and peace of mind because of her.

This was inconceivable to Madeleine. She had lived such a sober and retired life, never adorning her person, never appearing in public, nor listening to flattery, that she had no longer any idea of the impression she might make upon a man.

'Then,' said Jeannette, 'since he loves you so much, and will die if you refuse him, will you persist in closing your eyes and ears to what I say to you? If you do, it must be because you dislike the poor young fellow, and would be sorry to make him happy.'

'Do not say that, Jeannette,' answered Madeleine; 'I love him almost, if not quite, as much as my Jeannie, and if I had ever suspected that he thought of me in another light, it is quite possible that my affection for him would have been more passionate. But what can you expect? I never dreamed of this, and I am still so dazed that I do not know how to answer. I ask for time to think of it and to talk it over with him, so that I may find out whether he does this from a whim or out of mere pique, or whether, perhaps, he thinks it is a duty he owes me. This I am afraid of most of all, and I think he has repaid me fully for the care I took of him, and it would be too much for him to give me his liberty and himself, at least unless he loves me as you think he does.'

When Jeannette heard these words, she let down the corner of her apron, and François, who was waiting near at hand with his eyes fixed upon her, was beside them in an instant. The clever Jeannette asked Jeannie to show her the fountain, and they strolled off together, leaving Madeleine and François together.

But Madeleine, who had expected to put her questions to the waif, in perfect calmness, was suddenly covered with shyness and confusion, like a young girl; for confusion such as hers, so sweet and pleasant to see, belongs to no age, but is bred of innocence of mind and purity of life. When François saw that his dear mother blushed and trembled as he did, he received it as a more favourable token than if she had kept her usual serene manner. He took her hand and arm, but he could not speak. Trembling all the while, she tried to shake herself loose and to follow Jeannie and Jeannette, but he held her fast, and made her turn back with him. When Madeleine saw his boldness in opposing his will to hers, she understood, better than if he had spoken, that it was no longer her child, the waif, but her lover, François, that walked by her side.

After they had gone a little distance, silent, but linked arm in arm, as vine is interlaced with vine, François said:

'Let us go to the fountain; perhaps I may find my tongue there.'

They did not find Jeannie and Jeannette beside the fountain, for they had gone home; but François found courage to speak, remembering that it was there he had seen Madeleine for the first time, and there, too, he had bidden her farewell, eleven years afterwards. We must believe that he spoke very fluently, and that Madeleine did not gainsay him, for they were still there at midnight. She was crying for joy, and he was on his knees before her, thanking her for accepting him for her husband.

* * * * * * * *

'There ends the story,' said the hemp-dresser, 'for it would take too long to tell you about the wedding. I was present, myself, and the same day the waif married Madeleine in the parish of Mers, Jeannette was married in the parish of Aigurande. Jean Vertaud insisted that François and his wife, and Jeannie, who was happy as a king, with their friends, relations and acquaintances, should come to his house for the wedding-feast, which was finer, grander and more delightful than anything I have ever seen since.'

'Is the story true in all points?' asked Sylvine Courtioux.

'If it is not, it might be,' answered the hemp-dresser. 'If you do not believe me, go and see for yourself.'

NOTES

François the Waif was first published in French in 1848 as *François le Champi*; it was first published in this translation by Jane Minot Sedgwick in 1894. The text of this edition is based on that of the first publication in Sedgwick's translation. In some instances, spelling has been updated and made consistent, and punctuation has been silently corrected to make the text more appealing to the modern reader.

6   *feuilleton of the Journal des débats*: A French newspaper published between 1789 and 1944. Its feuilleton (a section of a newspaper given over to literature and criticism) was renowned.

6   *the final downfall… February 1848*: The 'July Monarchy' of Louis Philippe I (1773–1850), which lasted from the 26th of July 1830, under the July Revolution of 1830, until the 23rd of February 1848, ended by the Revolution of 1848.

6   *the beautiful plant called nénufar, or Nymphaea*: That is, water lilies.

8   *the shameful calling of beggars*: Published some 175 years ago, some of the attitudes in the text are now considered archaic and offensive.

12   *pianissimo… adagio of winter*: Musical terms: pianissimo (very softly); andante (moderately slow); adagio (slow).

14   *Petrarch has its relative beauty… birds*: References to: the Italian poet Petrarch (1304–74); Vaucluse, an area in the south-eastern French

region of Provence-Alpes-Côte d'Azur; Jacob van Ruisdael (*c*.1628–82), a Dutch landscape painter; the composer Wolfgang Amadeus Mozart (1756–91); and Philomel, a character in Greek mythology, daughter of the King of Athens, who was turned into a swallow or a nightingale.

16   *the primitive man of Jean-Jacques's dreams*: This is a reference to the philosopher and writer Jean-Jacques Rousseau (1712–78), who had much to say about human development.

17   *the language of the Academy*: The Académie Française is the foremost council for the French language, acting as the official authority on the language, and publishing the official dictionary.

17   *the shepherds of Longus down to those of Trianon*: Longus was the author of the ancient Greek romance *Daphnis and Chloe*; Trianon refers to an area of the Versailles estate, where Marie Antoinette and her courtiers would spend time dressed in the style of shepherds.

18   *shepherdesses of Astraea*: A reference to the monumental work *L'Astrée* by Honoré d'Urfé (1568–1625), published between 1607 and 1627, which revolves around two shepherds, Astrée and her lover Céladon.

18   *Lignon of Florian*: The Lignon is a French river; 'Florian' refers to the French writer and fabulist Jean-Pierre Claris de Florian (1755–94), who was noted for his pastoral poetry and novels.

18   *sabots*: A type of shoe, formed from a single, hollowed-out piece of wood, worn by French peasants.

18   *Sedaine*: This is a reference to the French dramatist Michel-Jean Sedaine (1719–97).

19   *The Devil's Pool*: That is, *La Mare au Diable*, an 1846 novel by Sand.

19   *Henri Meunier*: Henri Meunier (1873–1922) was a Belgian artist and designer of the belle époque.

21   *dog of Brisquet*: This is a reference to the children's story, the *Histoire du chien de Brisquet* by the French author Charles Nodier (1780–1844). The story was about a bichon dog.

22   *Montaigne*: That is, the French essayist Michel Eyquem de Montaigne (1533–92).